24

THE X

LORENA BATHEY

Linda!
Life is meant
to be kicked,
So put your boots
on! ♡
LB

Published by Lorena B Books
Release date December 2012

ISBN is 9780985488802

Cover Design by Josh May Media
Editing by Susy Flory and There for You Editing

THE X

by
LORENA BATHEY

LORENA B BOOKS PUBLISHING

THE X
CHAPTERS

For everyone that had to take a chance and become more than they thought they were.

ONE

Clarissa Hadonfield stretched. She felt her sore muscles. Her calves were tense. She strained to hear any sound out of the ordinary. Bryce had told her that the house was bugged. She was being listened to. It seemed astonishing that this was now her life and that she had a listening device in her bedroom. It was hard not to yell profanities and expletives into the mic located behind her headboard, instead she pushed the bed hard against the wall as she got up. Clarissa laughed silently, went into the bathroom, and began running the water. She looked at the bruise on her face. Bryce really caught her good when he kicked her. An hour later she had taken a shower and was ready to head out for the day. She picked up the bugged cell phone and called into work telling them she'd be out ill. Then she picked up her pre-paid cell and dialed Bryce's number.

Traveling north on the highway she finally turned west as she headed towards the ocean. She kept her speed just a few miles above the speed limit. The traffic was busy because it was commute hour, but the cars diminished the closer she got to the ocean. She turned quickly left and then made an immediate right onto a side street. She killed the engine and ducked down as a black sedan with no distinguishing marks drove past her. Clarissa took a mirror from her console and used the side mirror so she could see the black car. It was stopped at the end of the street, the driver's door open, and a man was standing next to the car talking into a phone while looking around.

Clarissa smiled and waited a minute more before raising her head. She saw the man get into the black sedan and take off with tires squealing. She started her engine and backed into a driveway to turn around. She headed back the way she came towards the ocean. Ten minutes later, she was pulling into the parking lot at Ocean Beach. She could see Bryce's truck halfway down the lot. She parked her car facing the ocean and waited. A minute later she heard a light tapping and saw Bryce's face in the window. She undid the lock and let him in.

"Drive. Slowly. I'll tell you where to go."

Clarissa started the motor and headed back to the highway. She could smell Bryce's clean and masculine smell and took in the pleasure of that heady scent. Some men just smelled good. Bryce didn't talk as they continued down the road. She looked at him and he turned towards her.

"Did you get what I told you to get?" He checked his watch.

"Yes. It's in my purse." Clarissa motioned towards the back seat. "In the envelope."

Bryce reached through the seats and brought her purse into his lap. He looked at Clarissa as if asking for permission to enter the inner sanctum of a woman's secrets.

Clarissa nodded. "It's okay, Bryce. Just go into the pocket. It's right there."

Bryce opened the purse looking afraid.

That made Clarissa chuckle. *The big ex-FBI private investigator is afraid of my purse.* Bryce brought the white envelope out and opened the flap. A thick pack of money was lying there as if awaiting orders.

"It's all here?" Bryce looked at Clarissa. "The whole amount?" He seemed to question her.

"Yes, it's all there." Clarissa responded annoyed.

"I know I told you I wouldn't ask but…." Bryce trailed off as Clarissa stared at him. "Okay, okay." He took the envelope and put it into his jacket pocket. "Turn right here."

Clarissa followed directions and turned right. Bryce guided her to turn a couple more times until she found herself sitting in front of the Legion of Honor museum. The view was a stunning panorama of San Francisco gleaming on one side, and the Golden Gate Bridge glinting with the rare occurrence of sun on the other. She looked at the bridge as she parked and waited. They both sat in silence for a moment.

"You're sure about this?" Bryce's eyes were steady.

"Yes, completely. I have to know it all. I have to know what I'm dealing with." She sighed. "I have to get my kids back."

 TWO

Eight months before, Clarissa had been the typical housewife running the busy world of two teenagers, a husband, and her part-time job. Clarissa wasn't a stunning beauty, she was more classically pretty. She had a curvaceous body which was more Marilyn Monroe than Madonna. Her hair was shoulder length and auburn. Her color was something she was vain about, making sure she had twice-monthly touchups to keep her grey from showing. She worked out to keep her figure in reasonable shape, but she was far from perfect and wouldn't be doing any hundred yard dashes anytime soon.

Being in her mid-forties meant she was not just battling wrinkles, but also hormonal changes that women her age had to wrestle with. Clarissa's wide eyes were deep brown with long lashes and many remarked that they were her best feature. She had high cheek bones and nice lips. However, Clarissa's beauty was more attributed to the fact that she was content with who she was.

Her world was her family and she enjoyed the lifestyle they lived. That morning she was preparing to head into San Francisco from the suburbs to shop after work. Her teenagers were running late, and she yelled up to them to hurry or they'd miss their ride to school.

In the kitchen, she had already made their lunches and was looking at her datebook making sure that she had their piano lessons and lacrosse meetings all down correctly. Her husband walked in and opened the refrigerator.

"Hi, honey." Clarissa turned to him. He ignored her and got milk out for his coffee. Clarissa stood up and went to put her arms around him and he tensed up and moved out of her grasp. Clarissa was stunned. "Is something wrong?"

"Hmmm…what?" Her husband stirred his coffee and held the newspaper in his hand seeming to be intently reading the front page.

Clarissa felt irritation rising, as it usually did with her husband. "I said, is something wrong?"

"No, why?"

Seriously. Does he think I'm an idiot? Clarissa thought. "Because I just tried to hug you and you shrugged me off. Did I do something?" She wasn't sure she hadn't done something and just didn't remember.

"No, you didn't. I have to go to work now." Her husband left the paper and the coffee cup on the counter, grabbed his jacket off the stool, and was out of the house before she could respond. She looked out the window as he backed his car down the driveway. He was on the phone and seemed to be shouting at someone.

Clarissa wasn't sure what his behavior was about, but it seemed to be happening more and more lately. They had been married a long time and sometimes there were bumps in the road. Clarissa had to face the fact that their marriage had seemed to be disintegrating even more in the last few months. If she was really truthful, they had been more like roommates for the last year and a half. Ben had become more withdrawn and ignored her most of the time. He didn't fight with her, just appeared ambivalent. This hurt almost more than if he yelled. At least if he yelled he cared. Yet even with his horrible behavior, she still loved him because he was the father of her children and they had a lot of time invested into this marriage. He probably was just going through some mid-life crisis thing.

Footsteps were stomping down the stairs as her son yelled out, "Mom. I can't find my cleats."

Clarissa picked them up from under the kitchen table and held them out as her eldest son turned into the kitchen.

He stopped his shout mid-sentence and said, "Oh, thanks. Mom, did you see my jersey?"

"Over there on the table. I washed it. Did you bring a snack for practice?"

Clarissa's sons were the joy of her life. No matter the state of her twenty-year marriage, her sons were fantastic individuals. Jeremy was seventeen and adorable. He had wavy brown hair and her brown eyes. He was tall for his age and she noticed that girls always stared at him. He loved sports and was the star of the high school lacrosse team. Sean was fifteen and brighter than most Rhodes scholars. He seemed to be a computer nerd, but he was utterly cute. He had the same eyes as his mother and brother, but his hair was a lot darker. This gave him a mysterious quality which added to his quiet nature. He was a still-water-running-deep individual. He loved playing piano and was an adept musician. He'd even composed a few songs for the high school symphony.

Clarissa adored them and they reciprocated in their teenage-boy way. They both looked more like her than their dad, although Sean's darker hair was the exact shade as his father's. The boys were about a year into cutting the apron strings and they didn't hug her as much as they used to. Clarissa was okay with that most of the time, but sometimes she wanted a cuddle on the couch. Jeremy had a girlfriend, so he spent most nights out with her. She seemed like a nice enough girl. But like most of the girls today, she was too forward and aggressive for Clarissa's tastes. Clarissa had a guarded liking of her.

The boys tore through the kitchen in a whirl of questions while grabbing missing items. Clarissa smiled. It wouldn't be long before they would be on their way in life, which sometimes seemed hard to believe. She wondered how they would survive without her daily maintenance. She sat down as the boy's yelled goodbye in unison and the front door slammed.

"Goodbye." Clarissa whispered.

She sat down with her coffee to think. She would be on her way to the florist shop she worked at part-time before going shopping in San Francisco. Working at this shop gave her the chance to be independent and work with flowers, which she absolutely loved. She was a member of the Garden Club, and her backyard had won awards twice. Green things made her happy. As she touched the petals of the roses on her kitchen table she looked around at the home she had made. She'd spent so many happy moments with her sons as they grew up in this house. She smiled remembering their first steps, falls down the stairs, and all the cuddles they had on the couch watching movies.

Her husband, Benjamin Hadonfield, was a self-made man who owned a company specializing in high-end investments and financial planning. Clarissa really wasn't sure of the particulars of what he did, nor did she really care. She only knew that they had a very substantial income.

She'd met Ben in her senior year of college. Her cousin went to NYU and Clarissa, on spring break, had been thrilled to get to spend an entire week enjoying the sights of New York. Her cousin, Bea, introduced her to a huge group of people who seemed to be from another world than Clarissa had ever experienced. Clarissa loved the bohemian and exciting world of New York, although she wasn't sure if she fit in. One night they had attended a party at the penthouse apartment of her cousin's best friend where Ben had approached her. She and Ben had spent the evening dancing to slow songs and drinking beer. It had been a beautiful night and she and Ben spent the rest of her stay visiting museums and going to concerts. He was hard to figure out. Sometimes he was attentive and romantic and others he seemed miles away. However, when the time came for her to leave Ben told her he wasn't sure he could let her go home to San Francisco without him.

Corresponding for months, one day she'd opened her apartment door and Ben was standing there with suitcase in hand. He had taken a job with an investment firm and requested to be sent to their San Francisco office. They dated until he proposed six months later. Ben was as close to perfect as Clarissa had ever seen. He was contained, smart, successful, and she felt she couldn't have found a better partner for herself. Both her parents liked him very much.

Once they got married they moved to downtown San Francisco living in a charming building with pre-war apartments. They both enjoyed the nightlife the city offered. Since Ben was doing well at his company they could try new restaurants, attend charity galas, and run with a crowd that was moving up the social ladder. Clarissa didn't really care about all that, but she did like the pretty clothes and the excitement of being part of the city's young elite. When she got pregnant, things changed and she only wanted to find a nice house in the suburbs and be a mom. Ben was fine with that and Clarissa felt that somehow it fit the persona he wanted to create for himself. Being married with children made people trust you, and that would help with the clients he wanted to land.

They found a lovely house in Palo Alto. It was an older house, but with gorgeous hardwood floors, bay windows, a huge backyard, and drafty bedrooms. They extensively renovated putting in French doors, new windows, and opening up the floor plan a bit. Before the baby came they even added a couple of rooms upstairs. Clarissa was sure they'd have a big family. She decorated the house in classic style adding in a few eclectic items here and there to give it character. Their home was warm, inviting, and thoroughly tasteful. When her boys were born she and Ben left the social whirl of San Francisco and became more entrenched with the Palo Alto elite.

Being a prominent town near a very expensive college meant that there was a large collection of intellectuals and businessmen that liked the image that Palo Alto presented. Ben was one of these men. He golfed with the dean of Stanford, a couple of judges, and three multi-millionaires. That's how he grew his financial practice as a lot of work gets accomplished on a golf course. Before the boys were one and three respectively, Ben was doing so well he started his own company. It grew by leaps and bounds, so Clarissa never had to worry about money. Ben was a workaholic, at least that's what Clarissa told herself, because he wasn't home very much. Of course, she believed he was doing all this hard work for her and the boys. But the truth was that after the boys were toddlers, Ben was not as involved in their lives as Clarissa would've liked.

This is when they started drifting apart. She was all about the kids, their activities, and helping them grow up. But Ben was all about work, work, and a little more work thrown in. The stoic quality Clarissa had seen while they were dating became the most prominent part of his personality. He rarely goofed around with her like before. Their time spent socializing was only with people Ben felt could progress his business. Clarissa didn't always like the people that Ben insisted they spend time with. She thought they were pretentious and Clarissa felt they didn't really seem to like her. Some of the individuals that Ben called his inner circle were heavily connected, particularly in government, which was odd since he'd always eschewed politics. But Clarissa went along, playing the doting wife role well. She never tried to embarrass Ben, although he would often make harsh comments to her under his breath about her behavior. She tried not to be embarrassed when others overheard the exchange and gave her pitying looks. Many evenings when he'd had too much to drink, she had to listen to a diatribe of her faults and imperfections as she drove them home.

As their boys went through middle school Ben was usually missing from recitals or games. Clarissa tried to make it up to the boys, but it was hard to be both parents. The boys were always trying to get Ben's attention on the weekends he was around. He spent little time with the boys, unless it was for father and son events at the country club when other men he hung around would bring their sons too. At these events Ben would turn on the fatherly charm. It made Clarissa kind of sick to her stomach to see the insincerity, but the boys were so excited to get any attention they ate it up.

When the boys started high school

they seemed to pull away from their dad as they found their own interests, friends, and lives. Clarissa was still involved making sure to know their friends, girlfriends, and parents of said individuals. She made sure homework got done, curfews were kept, and that they ate a least one meal a day that had four food groups in it. They were good boys who seemed to be heading for success and adventure. They both had started talking about colleges. Jeremy was sure to get a scholarship for sports and Sean really wanted to try to get into Julliard. Clarissa had met with their career counselors to make sure they were on track. Of course, going to a private college prep school was a good advantage over a lot of students, and when you combined that with a hefty financial account to pull from, it looked like their futures were both bright.

The doorbell rang and Clarissa shook herself out of her ruminations to answer the door. On the porch was a man wearing a uniform from the phone company.

He looked at the clipboard in front of him. "Clarissa Hadonfield?"

"Yes. May I help you? Is there an

outage or something?"

The man handed her an envelope. "You've been served."

"What?" Clarissa turned the envelope over in her hand and recognized the law offices her husband used for work.

The guy had run off as soon as she had taken the envelope. He jumped over her bushes and rounded the corner.

"Wait. Come back here." Clarissa yelled after him.

She felt warm, her face flushed, and her stomach did flips. Served? For what? She was trying to think if she had gotten any tickets she didn't remember paying or anything else that might have caused her to get into legal trouble. Scanning her brain she found nothing. She shut the door and opened the envelope while standing in the foyer. The blue legal document was deeply creased as if someone had run it along an edge before putting it into the envelope. She saw her name on the front page and began to read aloud.

"Benjamin Hadonfield vs. Clarissa Hadonfield. The party of Benjamin Hadonfield....wait...divorce? These are divorce papers. Oh my God. He's divorcing me?"

Clarissa felt shock moving through her and battling to beat out anger. After mere seconds, the anger turned into tears. "Without talking to me?"

She made her way to the kitchen stumbling on the hall carpet. Once in the kitchen, she found her purse and searched for her phone. She pushed the auto dial for her husband's number and waited. It rang a few times, then there was a click, and Clarissa started yelling. "Why am I standing here holding divorce papers? How could you do this?" Her voice faded off as Benjamin's message began. Clarissa hung up.

The sun was shining through the window and she could see her beautiful garden with its perfectly planned out messiness. Her roses were beginning to bloom and she remembered she should be fertilizing them soon. The tears were rolling down her face and in her stomach was a hole. A huge, gaping hole as if she had been shot with a gun. The image of the movie Terminator went through her mind. She felt like the liquid guy when he gets hit with the shotgun and there's a hole you can see through. That's how Clarissa's stomach felt. Empty, cold, and gaping.

She stood there looking out the window with questions racing through her mind. *What happened? I mean, I know what happened. But really divorced? He's divorcing me? How can that be? What will I do? Will I have to move?* Her mind was reeling and she had to sit down. She looked at her phone and thought about calling someone, but she didn't know who to call. The one person she wanted to talk to she didn't think was going to answer her.

Clarissa saw the time. "I have to go to work," she said aloud. She wasn't sure how she was going to function, but she knew sitting here waiting to find out what was going on was not going to be any better. For now, she had to just keep moving and doing what she knew and hopefully answers would come later.

Pulling into the parking lot in back of the floral shop she saw that Becky was here. *Thank God. I can talk to Becky*, Clarissa thought with huge relief.

As she walked through the back door, the aroma of flowers greeted and slightly calmed her. She hung up her coat and purse and donned the bright pink apron they wore while working. Clarissa felt as if she was walking through the surf at the ocean struggling to make her legs move. In the shop the soothing colors and beauty of the flowers eased the stunned pain she'd felt since answering the doorbell.

The flower shop was the best in Palo Alto, and 'everyone-who-was-anyone' got their arrangements here. It was filled with not only the best blooms, but also interesting objects 'd art, small paintings, soaps, candles, and all other sorts of knick-knacks for the cream of society to add to their floral purchases. The concrete floors were painted a deep teal color and the walls were wood-siding painted deep rust. There were distinctive chandeliers hanging throughout the shop. All the tables were worn wood, mismatched, and covered with expensive trinkets. The focus of the store was the enormous wood table that for many years must've had people eating meals around it, and now held two cash registers, ribbon, clear plastic for wrapping flowers, and stacks of receipts. Three women were working behind the desk. One a young college girl named Heather, who was fresh and pretty with blonde hair, blue eyes, and clear skin. The second was Liz, who was in her late-forties and starting over after her husband died. The third was Becky.

Clarissa breathed a sigh of relief when she saw Becky. Becky, or Rebecca Benito, was a force. She was tall, strong, and had long, massively curly, brown hair that looked a lot like a lion's mane. People always commented on her hair, but didn't always notice the eyes that saw through everybody. Becky grew up in Palo Alto and was from old family money, yet she was the most down-to-earth person Clarissa had ever met. Becky saw through the society women that came in here, and she never was a sycophant to their demands. While this probably should have ended her business, instead, she was hugely successful because everyone knew that Becky was fair and connected.

As Clarissa stood there taking in the store, Becky turned from the woman she was helping and her eyebrows drew together. "Excuse me, Mrs. Wallingford. I'm going let Heather finish taking care of you." Becky nodded towards the co-ed while Mrs. Wallingford's eyes filled with terror.

Heather bounced over and Becky walked towards Clarissa.

"Clarissa?" Becky came toward her and took her hand. "Follow me."

Clarissa let herself be led to Becky's office like a child. Walking through the shop to the back room, people started to ask questions until they saw Becky's face. Everyone knew her 'don't bother me' face and when she was wearing it you did just that. Becky pushed her office door open and pointed to the chair. Clarissa obeyed and sat down while Becky walked behind her desk saying, "Tell me everything."

Clarissa began to cry. "Oh God, Becky. Ben served me divorce papers this morning. A guy came to the door dressed like the phone guy and handed me the papers. I was shocked. I mean, Ben said nothing to me. And it's not like I don't know we haven't been doing great. But who does that without letting you know? Who just blindsides someone that they are supposed to love?"

"What a shithead." Becky got up and handed Clarissa a box of tissues. "Honey look, I know you aren't happy. While you might not admit it right now, this might all be for the best. I mean, you can't just go along in life like an ostrich pretending that everything is okay. And I know the boys fulfill most of your needs, but they can't be your whole life. You have to find something for yourself, and that means taking some chances. I know this feels like someone hit you in the gut, but, think for a minute. Just give it a second and think, could this be for the best?" She looked at Clarissa with a raised eyebrow.

Clarissa's sobs got louder and Becky's brows furrowed. "Really, Clarissa. Seriously? You think that maybe...."

Clarissa looked at Becky and sniffled. "I know. You might be right. And yes, if I'm honest, something had to give. But right now all I can think is what an asshole." She blew her nose loudly into a tissue.

Becky sighed. "That's because he is an asshole. Do the boys know?"

Clarissa shook her head. "No, it happened right after they left for school. What am I gonna tell them?"

Becky looked down at her desk. "They must know something is up. You and Ben, haven't been...well, you're not lovey dovey are you?"

"Not really. Not for a while. It's still

not going to be easy to tell them. And what do I say? Do I say that he blindsided me? Should I be honest and tell them about him or do I just keep them happy?" Clarissa was shaking her head.

"Well, if it were me I'd tell them the truth. The truth is always best. But with kids, you gotta be careful 'cause you don't want to look like you are trying to get them to take sides, you know. Do you have a lawyer?"

Clarissa's eyes were moist again. "No. Where do I even find one? Ben took the only one I know and because he does business with Ben, he won't consider me. I don't handle the money, Ben does. I'm not even sure what to do."

"Come on." Becky got up and took off her apron. She grabbed her purse and took Clarissa's hand. As she moved to the back exit she yelled she'd be back later. Taking Clarissa's coat and purse, Becky handed them to her and they walked towards Becky's car. She unlocked the door and said, "Clarissa, we're gonna take the bull by the horns. Best way to handle the situation."

Twenty minutes later Becky pulled up to her parent's palatial home. Becky's background was lots of old money, prestige, and notoriety. Her parents were in their seventies and were the social elite of the area. But like Becky, they were real people that took no crap from anyone. Becky's dad was a judge and her mom had been a professor at Stanford. They were smart people and a heck of a lot of fun. Clarissa had been to many parties at their home and it was the one thing about Becky that Ben had liked. It had made Ben happy that Clarissa socialized with someone like Becky and her parents.

Entering the house was like going to a museum. Not only was the house immense, but it was beautifully decorated with French antiques and modern art of the likes of Jackson Pollock. This eclectic mix made it more than just a fine home of rich people, it made it interesting, just like the people who inhabited it.

"Dad? Where are you?" Becky yelled from the front door.

"Sugar lamb, that you?" Becky's mom was from the south and her accent was soft and buttery, but her demeanor was strong and unyielding.

"Hey, mom. Dad here?"

"He's in the office. I'm making flan, you want some?"

Becky laughed. "My mom, the southern belle, is making flan. Rosa, our maid, showed her how and now she makes it every week. Weirdo." Becky cupped her mouth and yelled towards the back of the house, "Okay, mom, we'll be back there in a minute. Clarissa is with me."

"Hello, Clarissa, dear." Becky's mom yelled back.

Clarissa smiled at this yelling match of pleasantries occurring in the stately mansion.

Becky led the way down the hallway to a gorgeous, cherry wood door. Pushing it open she said, "Daddy-o, you here?"

A grey-haired man sat behind the biggest desk Clarissa had ever seen. There was a huge, ornate gold lamp on the table, an old typewriter, and an enormous crystal decanter of what was probably whiskey. Rodolfo Benito was a big man. He had a huge mane of white hair, a sharp Italian nose, and bright blue eyes. His presence was that of a man who knew who he was, what he was here to do, and how to go about getting it done. Being a judge made him connected politically and socially, but being Rodolfo Benito made him someone you didn't mess with. He had a huge laugh, a big heart, and keen intellect. And more than anything he loved his girls, who were the pride of his life.

"Becks, my sweet petunia, come give your dad a kiss." He stood up from the desk. At six-foot-four he was tall and broad. There was no way to miss this man in a room.

Becky headed to the desk with her arms out. "Hey Daddy-o. Remember Clarissa?" The words were muffled as her father folded her into a big hug.

Rodolfo looked over his daughter's head and smiled at Clarissa. He took in her face in a way that might have been scary if she had been standing in his courtroom, but here in his office it was simply inquiring. "What's the matter, buttercup?"

Becky pulled back and hit him in the chest. "How do you do that? I swear you should be on the psychic network. It's Clarissa. She needs your help."

"Sit down, Clarissa. You want a belt?" He pulled the stopper off the decanter and poured double shots into two glasses.

"No. No...thank you. That's okay."

Clarissa was waving the drink away.

Rodolfo handed it to her. "Take it, sweetie. I think you can use it. Now…." He sat back down in the enormous leather chair, settled in, and looked at Clarissa. "Tell me how I can help."

Clarissa felt the tears starting. She took a drink from the glass and swallowed. The whiskey was old and smooth, that much she knew because it barely burned going down her throat. Like most drinks that are poured small and strong, it immediately caused her chest to warm. She took another sip and cleared her throat. Rodolfo's eyes never left her, and she could feel the fatherly concern.

Becky couldn't wait anymore. "Dad, this is the scoop. Clarissa is married to Benjamin Hadonfield. You heard of him? He's been here before to one or two of your soirees. Have you ever met him?"

"Hadonfield, I know him. He plays golf with some big wigs in the political game. Big hitters with questionable ethics. He seems to do well for a lot of his clients. But there has always been a whisper about him. Not that he's shady per se, but that there are secrets being kept. I don't know the secrets, just heard the gossip. Anyway, what happened? He beat you?"

Clarissa took another sip. Becky interjected. "He served her with divorce papers this morning. Totally blindsided her and she's still reeling. Anyway, she doesn't know the law and is scared. I thought you could help. They only have a business attorney and Clarissa doesn't do any of the money, so what should she do? You know anyone who can help?"

Rodolfo stood and brought the decanter to Clarissa. He nodded his head towards her glass and she smiled and held it up. "Dear, here's what we got. Just knowing these facts, the scuttle about town, and the weasely way he did this and I would think... mistress. Also pretty sure he's been hiding the cash. Do you know where all the money is?"

Clarissa shook her head. The whiskey was doing its job making her not care about anything, even the possible devastation of her life.

"So what does she do, Dad?"

Rodolfo leaned against the desk and said, "Hon, you need to look at me."

Clarissa felt a bit like a child with Becky's father. It was almost like she was in high school and getting in trouble instead of being a forty-something-year-old woman facing the ending of her marriage and life. She looked up. "Yes?"

"You better prepare for battle. This man, what I know of him, is aggressive and pretty cutthroat. That means that since he's been planning this whole thing and you've known nothing about it, you're gonna feel the full brunt of his sneaky ways and you're easy prey. Think little white bunny caught in a huge metal trap." He stopped, took a sip of whiskey, cleared his throat, and smiled at her. "That being said, you came to the right place. The only way to fight a battle is to prepare, practice, and arm yourself. So that's what you need to do. Realize that now you have the papers you have to go into survival mode. He plans to take you down. You don't do a surprise attack without wanting total annihilation of your enemy."

Clarissa threw back the rest of her whiskey. "What do I do?"

"First, you got to get a good lawyer. I have several I would recommend, but given the circumstances, Mary Ann Marchesa would be my bet. She's a teeny little thing, but she will take you down. She has a bit of an issue with men which can work to your advantage. She's not cheap, but lawyer fees will be part of what she will get for you in the settlement." Rodolfo went back to his desk, opened a drawer and pulled out the biggest rolodex Clarissa had ever seen. He moved through the cards, found what he wanted, and wrote a number down on a piece of paper.

"Dad, what should she do? I mean, like right now. Should she go to the bank and take money out? What?" Becky seemed to be nervous for Clarissa.

"Do you have access to your bank accounts?"

"Yes. And I have credit cards."

"Okay, then go to your bank and get as much cash out as you can. Then head to the banks the credit cards are issued with and get all the cash advances you can. Once you get the cash, you need to hide it somewhere safe. I would recommend getting a safety deposit box. Then go shopping and purchase bigger items that can be returned for cash. Jewelry is good and right now buy heavy, thick gold pieces since the rate for gold is high and you can sell them for what you pay for them." He returned to his rolodex and wrote another number down. "This is a jeweler I know very well. Just look at Lorraine's fingers and neck to see our intimate relationship. He will help you out if you need to sell anything. Do you have pieces you can sell now?"

Clarissa took a mental inventory of her jewelry. She had a few pieces, especially the diamonds Ben always gave her for any five years they were together. She figured she had a lot more than she remembered. She nodded.

"Basically, you need to consolidate as much as you can. Cash is going to be your friend, especially if you can hide it. He is going to try to screw you financially, that much is for sure. So you need to think differently. I've seen it many times." Rodolfo came close to Clarissa, took her glass, and set it on the desk. He took her hands in his and looked at her. "Clarissa, the person you thought you knew, the man you believed you were married to, he is no longer there. He doesn't have guilt or remorse. He doesn't care if you're going to be okay. Basically, he is ready to discard you. That means you're not safe. Do you understand?"

Clarissa could feel the strength in his

hands. He wasn't kidding and he wasn't sugarcoating this. She was in trouble and she needed to be ready. "I understand. But the kids?"

"Is he close to them?"

"Not really. I mean he pretends to be, but they don't spend much time with him unless it's to show them off in some way."

Rodolfo was thinking. "How old are they?"

"Jeremy is seventeen and Sean is fifteen."

"Well there won't be long child support because it will end when they are over eighteen. But the alimony would be substantial given the years you've been married and his income level. Have you ever worked outside of the home?"

"Well, I work at Floration now. I did work the first few years we were married. But once I had the boys, I stopped and stayed home."

"That's good. That means that you will probably get spousal support until he is at least sixty-five. And he'll have to pay you enough to sustain your lifestyle. Not as much as you think, but it could be enough. Listen, you need to go and do what I said.

Get the cash from wherever you can and don't tell anyone where it is. Okay?"

"Yes, I understand, Mr. Benito."

"Call me Rodolfo."

Clarissa smiled. "Thank you, Rodolfo. Thank you so much. I don't know...." Clarissa looked at Becky. "Thank you, Becky for bringing me here."

"Of course. I agree with my dad. You need to stockpile the cash. Ben knows money and probably knows how to hide money too. So you need to get yourself protected as soon as possible. But not before some flan." Becky hugged her dad. "Thanks daddy-o. You're the bee's knees."

"You're welcome, Muffinhead. Better go eat some of your mom's flan or she'll be pushing it down my throat. I love flan as much as the next guy, but I am seriously sick of it."

Becky and Clarissa stood up. Clarissa felt the whiskey when she did and swayed a bit. "Umm...."

Rodolfo chuckled. "Don't worry; it's good to feel that way now. Enjoy it! Oh, and take some flan home with you too!"

Three

After meeting with Rodolfo, Clarissa had done exactly what he'd told her to do. She cleared out the joint bank accounts which netted her over twenty thousand dollars. She set up a new account in her name at a small local bank and rented a safety deposit box. Becky had gone with her and kept saying things to keep Clarissa focused, tough, and moving forward. They put five hundred dollars in the bank account and the rest went into the safety deposit box. Clarissa had also gone to the three banks where their credit cards had been issued and did the maximum cash advances which netted her another fifty thousand dollars also nestled in the safety deposit box.

She called Mary Ann Marchesa and set up an emergency meeting with her. Rodolfo had called her so she fit Clarissa into her schedule. Mary Ann was exactly as Rodolfo had described. She was only five feet two inches, yet she was powerful and angry, which could be a ruthless combination. Clarissa was glad she was on the same side as Mary Ann. But even being petite and sinewy, Mary Ann knew she was a woman and used that to her advantage whenever possible. She had agreed whole heartedly with Rodolfo that Clarissa's soon to be ex-husband was going for the jugular. Mary Ann took the case and Clarissa paid her retainer in cash from the safety deposit box.

Ben hadn't come home again after the morning Clarissa had been served with papers. He didn't respond to her phone or text messages in the following days and her emails went unanswered. She was angry and hurt, but trying to stay in a place which would allow her to protect herself and the boys. She had told the boys what happened. At first they were surprised that their dad hadn't come home to see her. They told her that Ben had shown up at school the day she got the papers to explain his side to them. Now months had passed and the boys were on a schedule of spending every other weekend with their dad and staying home with Clarissa during the week. They seemed to be doing well, though they both had gotten quieter with her. She figured that was from the emotional turmoil they must be going through.

One night at dinner she bit the bullet and asked the boys. "What exactly was his side?" Clarissa was very interested to know what Ben was thinking. While she didn't want to use her boys to get information, she needed to understand what Ben was planning.

Jeremy shrugged his shoulders. "He said your marriage was dead and you both decided to put this all behind you and start over again. He said you weren't mad at him and that you both were in agreement on how things should be."

Clarissa dug her nails into her palms holding back a nasty expletive. "Really, that's what he said, huh?"

Sean was looking at his mother, "Isn't

that true, Mom?"

"Well…." Clarissa didn't know what to say. Should she create an antagonistic view of Ben to the boys or should she keep quiet knowing that her attorney was going to do what needed to be done? She really didn't know the right thing to do. She thought that telling them that their father was a horse's ass might not be the best way to talk about their father, but she was tired of him lying while she tried to be a bigger person. She heard Becky's dad in her head and decided that the truth was always the best thing. Her boys knew she wasn't vindictive and they would understand. It would be better in the end, because after they heard how he treated her they might get it. She responded quietly, "That's not totally true, Jeremy."

Jeremy stopped eating and Sean set his fork down. "What do you mean, Mom? What isn't true?"

"Your dad and I did not come to an agreement about this together. I was served divorce papers at the front door and had no idea it was coming. He hasn't spoken to me since the morning the divorce papers came. And he has never explained anything to me about why." Clarissa looked up expecting to see sympathy in her boy's eyes. But Jeremy had none and Sean was staring at his napkin. "What?"

Jeremy spoke first. "Dad said you'd say that. He said that he's been unhappy for years and has been asking you for a divorce over and over, but you wouldn't give it to him. He said he's been miserable for a long time and you've been really mean to him."

"What?" Clarissa stopped and took a breath to calm down. "Jeremy, that's absolutely untrue. I have been the same person I have always been. I loved…love your dad and did everything I could to help his business and make his life wonderful. Just like with you boys."

Sean looked up. "Mom, you're a great mom and Dad agrees with that. He just says you guys haven't had a marriage in a long time. Like, you know." Sean rolled his eyes.

Clarissa was having a hard time keeping calm. She looked at the boys she had raised from crying infants to curly-headed toddlers, and saw them as the men they were becoming. She also understood that Ben had been playing more dirty than she believed he would. He was turning the boys against her. How did she combat this without looking pathetic and pleading?

"Okay, here's the truth. Your father has decided to end our marriage without speaking to me. He has hidden all our assets so that I have no money at my disposal except for a small amount. He will not take my calls and has been vicious with my attorney." She took another breath and looked at the boys. "I have been home raising you both your whole life. My job at the floral shop will not support my life. I am beholden to your father and believed that he would be gracious and generous, and he is being neither. That's the truth. Why would I lie?"

Jeremy got up from the table and put his dish in the sink. "Why would you tell the truth?"

"Jeremy Lincoln Hadonfield, how dare you talk to me like that? Put your dish in the dishwasher right now." Clarissa was livid with his disrespect and frightened that he sounded a lot like Ben.

"No. You do it." And he walked out of the kitchen.

Clarissa looked at Sean, who still had his head bowed at the table.

"Sorry, mom." He got up and washed his plate and put both the plates in the dishwasher as Clarissa sat down at the table.

She was enraged and didn't know what to do with it. Thinking about the way the whiskey had felt that day at the Benito's she went into the den, found a Waterford crystal glass, opened a bottle, and poured herself half a glass. She took the first sip too fast and started to cough. Tears came to her eyes as her thoughts raced. *He got to the boys. He's out to destroy me.* She finished the glass and poured another, feeling the delicious easing of her muscles, her mind, and her heart. She sat down at his desk and cursed him under her breath. "Asshole."

It was then she thought to go through the desk. She opened drawers and looked at papers, files, receipts, and cards. Nothing seemed to jump out at her and most of the financial paperwork was like reading Greek. She kept sipping and searching looking for something that would make sense to her. After an hour and another glass of whiskey, she was feeling calmer and warmer but still hadn't found anything. That was when she noticed a receipt caught in the corner of the drawer. She eased it out. It was a credit card receipt and she saw there were tickets to Idaho, new furniture, rent for a condo, and a car. Wait, a car? There was a down payment on his American Express for a Chevy Camaro. *Oh my God, he bought Jeremy a car. That's why Jeremy is acting like this.*

Clarissa set the receipt down. He'd done all this before he'd left. He had bought the car before. He'd intended to get the boys away from her. Clarissa shook her head thinking, what better way than to buy them?

She walked upstairs and knocked on Jeremy's door. He didn't answer so she turned the knob and opened the door. Jeremy was sitting on the bed with a new iPad, wearing expensive looking headphones and watching a movie. "Jeremy."

Jeremy didn't respond.

Clarissa said it louder, "Jeremy."

But still he didn't hear her. Those headphones must be really loud. Clarissa walked to his bed and touched his shoulder.

He jumped and growled at her. "What?"

"Where did you get that?" She pointed at the iTouch.

"Dad."

"Really? Did he also buy you a car?"

"Um...." Jeremy now seemed nervous.

"Jeremy, did your father buy you a

Chevy Camaro and then tell you not to tell me?"

"He got me a car. He didn't say directly not to tell you, but he said you'd take it away if you knew I had it. Said you didn't want me to have a car or even drive until I was eighteen." Jeremy frowned looking angry with Clarissa.

"Jeremy, I never said any of that. Why do you believe what he's telling you? I've always been honest with you, haven't I?" Clarissa was beside herself seeing the anger and irritation in her son's eyes. "If you wanted a car I wouldn't have said no."

"Right, mom. You barely let me drive even though I have my license. Dad's right, you're afraid of everything."

"What? I'm not afraid of everything." Clarissa immediately began calculating her fears in her head.

"Whatever. Anyway, dad got me a car and I get to drive it at his house. So there's no real reason to tell you anyway."

"Jeremy, I don't know who you think you are talking to. I'm your mother and you're being incredibly rude and nasty. Why would you do that to me? I've always helped you. Loved you. Why are you now acting like this angry teenager who hates his mother?"

"Cause maybe I am an angry teenager who hates his mother!" Jeremy yelled and Clarissa felt assaulted by the words.

She stood there and stared at him. "What?"

Jeremy seemed to falter a bit watching her eyes tear up. "Mom...."

"You hate me? Really? You really hate me? How is that possible?" Clarissa turned and walked towards the door. When she reached the threshold she turned to Jeremy. "Well, I love you. I love you with all my heart and I always will. There's nothing you can do or say that will change that. So if you need to be angry with me about this and need to believe that you hate me, then there is nothing I can do about that. But know this, I love you, Jeremy."

She closed the door behind her and walked slowly towards her room. As she passed Sean's room she looked through his open door. He was sitting at his desk with an iPad in front of him and he'd obviously heard the whole exchange. His face was stoic and he looked as if he might be crying, but he didn't move towards Clarissa. This lack of support felt as if he'd emotionally slapped her. Before he usually would've run to her and told her that he loved her. She paused for a moment waiting, but Sean stayed still. She continued to her room.

That night she barely slept. The next morning she lay in her bed listening to the boys getting ready for school and didn't go down to make their lunches like she usually did. When the front door slammed, she got up and went to the kitchen. She looked at the coffee maker and instead went to the den, grabbed the whiskey bottle from the desk, the receipt, and went to sit at the kitchen table.

"Mary Ann Marchesa, please." She stopped to take a slug of whiskey. She never thought about the fact that she was drinking first thing in the morning. She was still shell-shocked from the revelations from her sons.

"Hey, Clarissa, how are you? I just got a brief from Benjamin's attorney today. Um…." Mary Ann stammered.

Clarissa took another drink. "Let me guess, he's asking for full custody of the boys."

"Yes. How did you know? Did he tell you?" Mary Ann seemed truly puzzled.

"No, I figured it out. Last night I heard what Ben's scheme has been. He's been luring the boys away buying them things. He bought Jeremy a car and gave them both new iPad's with expensive headphones. He's bribing them, Mary Ann."

"That jerk. I mean it, he's really low. Sorry, I probably shouldn't have said that, it's not very professional of me."

"But true, Mary Ann, very true! So do I have any options?" Clarissa was feeling pretty numb from her liquid breakfast.

"Well, he's gonna have to prove that you shouldn't have custody of the boys. That's going to be impossible given everything you've done for them. And of course we have plenty of witnesses that will attest to your parenting ability. But...." Mary Ann trailed off.

"What?" Clarissa heard the tone in Mary Ann's voice. "What?"

"Well, the boys are of an age where the judge might talk to them directly. What they say about you and what they want will weigh heavily in his decision. Because the boys are older, the judge might simply rule the way they want. But we have a process to go through so you'll just have to be patient."

Clarissa felt fear. "How can that be? I mean, they're still children."

"Yes, that's true and by law they can't really choose. But in regards to children of this age it's different than if they were six and seven. They're old enough to make decisions and share their feelings. The judge can take their feelings and with the rest of the situation, well...I have to be honest with you. Clarissa, Benjamin is highly connected. He knows a lot of people in politics, even a few judges. If he gets the right judge, while they should recuse themselves, they don't have to. Benjamin could get his way. I have to tell you the facts and prepare you for what could happen." Mary Ann seemed afraid of the silence on the other end. "Clarissa, are you there? You okay? Do you have someone that could stay with you today?"

"No, it's okay. I'm alright. I have to go. Got to go to work. I'll talk to you later." Clarissa hung up the phone and ran up the stairs. She put on a pair of blue velour sweats, lipstick, fluffed her hair and headed out the front door. Jumping into her Mercedes sedan she backed out of the driveway. She didn't have a destination; she simply knew that if she stayed in that house one more minute, she would lose it. She headed to Becky's house knowing she was off today. As Clarissa drove down El Camino Real she saw a big sign that caught her eye and she turned abruptly into the driveway.

Sitting in her car looking in the window at the men in robes with black belts tied around their waists, she watched them moving in unison and the look on their faces held her attention. She grabbed her purse and got out of the car moving through the door quietly. The sound hit her. She hadn't thought it would be noisy. But the men were yelling gutturally and striking forward with a roar. Clarissa sat down on the plastic chair and observed.

Twenty-minutes later she was leaning her head in her hands watching with fascination as the men moved with purpose, strength, and basically were kickass. The class ended and she stood. All of the men but two picked up their things and headed out the door. One man went to change in the back and one man began doing a dance of moves in front of the mirror.

"Excuse me." Clarissa felt timid after the sounds that she had just heard.

The man turned towards her. He was

striking with dark grey hair and blue eyes. He was tall and had long arms. Clarissa could see he was strong even though he wore a baggy black robe. He walked with grace and determination. There was no hesitation about him. He was all man, all muscle, and partly animalistic in his gaze. It wasn't leering, he was simply sizing up this forty year-old housewife standing in his dojo.

"Can I help you?" He moved closer to her and Clarissa took a step back.

"I was interested in learning what you were just doing."

"You want to learn karate?" He raised his eyebrows at her. "Do you have any previous experience?"

Clarissa was just about to say she took kickboxing at the club but realized how stupid that would sound. "No. I have no experience."

"Okay. We have classes every night. You start at white belt and move up the ranks by belts."

"Can you teach me right now?"

"Now? I guess...I have another class in a half an hour. And if you take personal lessons it's more than the group lessons."

He walked to the counter and handed her a price list.

Clarissa reached in her purse and pulled out a hundred dollar bill. "Will this cover a private lesson?"

He smiled. "Yes, it will. I'm Dan. And you are?"

"Clarissa."

Dan put his hands together knuckles facing each other turned towards the American flag and bowed from the waist. Then he stepped from the floor of the mat to the carpet of the waiting room, made the same hands, and bowed to the empty room."This way, Clarissa."

 FOUR

Two months later Clarissa was testing for her green belt. She had worked hard with Dan. She had started the day she walked into the dojo taking a half-hour lesson. Clarissa loved how exhausted and powerful it made her feel. She had continued by taking two or three lessons a week. The training was grueling and often humiliating. Clarissa had always thought she was in sorta good shape from working out regularly at the club, but doing karate was something completely different. Besides the cardio and strength, it took a mental edge that she had to work hard on. This is what had saved her during the last few months of the divorce proceedings and dealing with the boys. The karate also gave her a sense of power which made her realize that she could battle her ex for the boys. The training was building a strong resolve in her to not just fight, but to win.

After the fight with Jeremy, he had stopped coming home. Sean still came every week and sometimes stayed on her weekends, but he always arrived with a new tech gadget, game, or video. He spent the majority of their time together watching television or going out with his friends, so Clarissa had less and less time alone with him. It broke her heart not to see Jeremy, but she didn't give up. She called and left a message for him every morning and night to say good morning and good night respectively. Clarissa told him he was always welcome at home, no questions asked. And she ended every message with 'I love you.' He still hadn't spoken to her but that didn't matter. She needed to say the words everyday to survive how much she missed him.

Clarissa and Ben had their court date three months after Jeremy left. It was uncanny how on target Rodolfo had been with his assessment of what Ben would do. There didn't seem to be a mistress, but he'd closed their credit cards and checking accounts. No amount of snooping brought any new information to Clarissa. The only thing she had was the receipt she'd found in Ben's desk. She'd shown Mary Ann and asked if she could use it in her defense, but Mary Ann was solemn as she told Clarissa that Ben had pulled a judge that was a golfing buddy of his which meant she didn't think much was gonna go Clarissa's way.

That wasn't because of lack of fight. Mary Ann was a bull terrier that once attached to Ben's neck never let up. She hounded him about alimony, hiding the money, his callousness, and the kids. But he seemed to never rattle and everything Mary Ann brought up was objected to by his attorney and sustained by the judge. When they walked out of the courtroom Benjamin Hadonfield had full custody of the boys, only had to pay his ex-wife a pittance, and had taken over the house for a ridiculously small settlement to Clarissa.

Clarissa had almost thrown up when the verdict was read by the judge. All throughout the trial she'd been looking at Ben trying to catch his eye. She realized how cold he was and how dead his eyes seemed to be. His dark brown hair was severely cut and while he was thin, there was a soft, squishiness to his body. He looked weak, especially where his chin seemed to disappear into his neck. Clarissa looked to see if he ever looked at her with some sort of compassion. He never did. Even at the end he was stoic, shook his attorney's hand, and left the courtroom.

"Ben, how could you do this?" Clarissa had yelled as he walked towards the courtroom door.

He barely looked at her as he paused for a mere second with his hand on the door. "Easily." And he left.

Mary Ann stood looking at the door. "What a cold hearted…." The phrase didn't need to be uttered as the thought was shared by both the women.

Clarissa had left the courthouse, rented a u-haul and had gone home to pack up all her things and take some of the boys' memories for them to have in the future. She pulled all the furniture she was taking with her into the garage so the guys coming tomorrow could load it up. There wasn't much she wanted now from this home. Then she fell asleep in the den after her third glass of whiskey. Waking up in the morning with her head on the desk, she shuddered once and walked out to her potting shed. She filled up her wheelbarrow with bags of manure and wheeled it into the house. This was where she had raised her boys, loved her husband, and created a home, but now it was nothing to her.

The wheelbarrow creaked under the weight of all the manure it carried. Clarissa took the shovel and spread the manure over every rug, piece of furniture, and in every corner of every room of the house. She filled Ben's closet floor with it and then put all the rest of his expensive suits, ties, underwear, shoes, and cuff links in the middle. She threw buckets of water over it making an unholy mess that stunk horribly. When the doorbell rang she showed the guys the furniture that needed to be loaded into the U-Haul and went back to her task. By the time they left to meet at the Benito's she had finished by throwing Ben's rare book collection on the pile of stinking manure on the floor in the den. She had left the best for last.

Stopping to refill the wheelbarrow, she went to the garage. Her Mercedes was at Becky's so there were two empty spots. But the other three spots contained Ben's Corvette, Ferrari, and his beloved Aston Martin. Clarissa felt a little bit bad ruining the Aston Martin, but it had to be done. She filled each car's interior with manure. Then she brought the hose from outside and added water. The stench was horrific and the mess was worse. Clarissa smiled as the ooze she had concocted began to leak out the doors. She left the hose running, shut the garage door, changed her clothes in the guest bathroom, and headed to the U-Haul.

Becky had almost pee'd her pants laughing when Clarissa told her what she'd done. It was a classic move and something that Ben would never have suspected she'd have the guts to do. But Clarissa was not the same after the verdict. She understood that Ben had quietly and with complete purpose stole her boys and destroyed her world. Any emotion she ever had for him was gone. Now it was about survival and finding a way to get her boys back.

The Benito's had been amazing. They

had a guest house that they let her have rent free. It was a charming bungalow with its own driveway and garage. Rodolfo and Lorraine were heading off for an extended trip to Europe so Clarissa was going to watch the property to help them out. She had full privileges of the main house if she wished, including the hot tub, steam, and sauna. After they left she settled in spending most of her time working at Floration and taking karate classes.

One night after sparring with Dan, she asked him if he wanted to go grab a drink. It wasn't motivated by interest in him romantically as much as the need for another human being to talk to. They sat at the bar in a local restaurant which was pretty empty on a Tuesday night. After their second drink, Clarissa told Dan everything Ben had done. Dan couldn't believe how heartless he'd been, especially about taking the boys away.

He shook his head. "Sounds like he paid them off."

"Yes, I think that's true. I don't want to believe that my boys can be bought. But I can't deny that they're gone. It seems amazing to me that one day you can open your door to the phone guy and a bomb drops on your life. So here I sit. I may be stronger physically and emotionally, but without the people in the world who mean most to me." Clarissa paused and took a sip of her beer. "And I think there's something else here. I can't put my finger on it. Call it women's or mother's intuition, but something is wrong. I found a receipt that was the only proof that I have that something shady is going on. Besides the car he bought Jeremy, there were tickets for three to Idaho for a few months from now. I would assume it's for Ben and the boys, but why Idaho? He's never been there and doesn't have any family there that I know of. It's weird."

Dan held his beer and paused before saying, "Clarissa, you ever thought of hiring someone to get to the bottom of what's going on?"

She looked at Dan and nodded. "Of course I've thought about it. I guess I just figured it wouldn't solve anything. But this nagging feeling about that receipt is making me think it might be a good idea." Clarissa swallowed a sip of beer quickly. "Why? Do you know someone?"

"I don't usually tell people a lot about my past, especially students. But, I'm really impressed by how hard you've been working and now hearing the story behind it I think I can trust you. I can right?"

"What? Trust me?" Clarissa crossed her heart. "Absolutely."

Dan signaled the bartender to refill their drinks. "I'm ex-FBI."

Clarissa smiled, "I figured it had to be something like that."

"Oh, it's that obvious is it?"

"Well, I figured you were either military or a cop."

Dan nodded at the bartender when he set down their new beers. "I left the bureau a few years ago. I retired."

Clarissa saluted her beer at Dan. "Thanks."

"No problem. Anyway, I worked a lot of places and finally got tired of the lifestyle. And in the bureau we have a pretty good retirement package. So, I took advantage of that and settled here."

"Are you from here?"

"No, I grew up in Oregon. But I like this area and didn't want to live in the city. I've wanted to open a studio somewhere and I thought there was enough money around here for people to afford classes. My buddy left a little bit after me. He stayed in the area and hung out a shingle."

"And you think he can help me?" Clarissa was hopeful. She took a long sip of her beer.

"Yep. He did a lot of intelligence stuff. You know, watch lists and stuff like that, and he was really connected. I'm sure he still is. So he should be able to help in getting information. Plus, he cross-trained with many of the military branches, so he has some real skills there." Dan reached into his wallet and pulled out a card handing it to Clarissa.

Clarissa looked at the plain white card with *Bryce Brightman* written in embossed black letters. The circle of gold and the writing made her think it looked like the cards you saw in the movie from FBI agents. "Bryce Brightman. Okay, thanks so much, Dan. I'll give him a call tomorrow. I better get going. I appreciate all your help and this." She held up the business card. "I'll let you know what happens at my next lesson."

Dan stood up. "I'll walk you to your car."

Clarissa noticed he had an almost full beer. "Don't be silly. You haven't finished your beer. I'll be fine. I have a green belt in karate." She smiled at him and tapped him on the back as she walked out of the bar.

The next day she called the number on the card and waited for Bryce Brightman to answer, but only got a message machine. She left her name, how she had found him, and asked for a call back. An hour later he called and asked to meet her for coffee to hear the specifics.

Clarissa was nervous as she pulled into the coffee store parking lot. She never had met a private detective before and wasn't sure what to do. Entering the store she wore her sunglasses while looking around for the man fitting the description he'd given her. A man sitting in the corner looked at her and nodded. She made her way over to his table.

"Mrs. Hadonfield?" His voice was deep and warm.

Clarissa sat down at the table. "Please, call me Clarissa."

He extended his hand. "Bryce Brightman, ma'am."

Clarissa took his hand and winced.

"Please, if you ever want me to hire you don't ever call me ma'am again."

"Sorry, force of habit. You really aren't a ma'am." His demeanor was hard to read but held innate strength which made Clarissa immediately sure of him.

"I'm sorry but I expected you to be a lot older. Closer to Dan's age."

"Oh. No, I'm fifty. Dan's in his sixties, I think."

"I thought you'd have to be older to retire."

Bryce shook his head. "No." He paused and Clarissa felt he wasn't telling her everything and that there was probably a story there.

"I started this private investigation stuff. It's pretty good since I have a lot of people who knew me when I worked a desk in San Francisco. I stay busy. "

"I guess I misunderstood. I thought you'd have to be in your sixties to retire."

"In the bureau you can retire at fifty on full pension."

"I see. Dan said you might be able to help me."

Bryce nodded towards the coffee counter. "Would you like a cup of coffee?"

"Yes, thank you. Decaf café au lait, please."

Bryce moved to the counter and Clarissa took that moment to check him out. He was tall, broad shoulders, but thinner than Dan. He had black hair with a smattering of grey in it. He moved confidently and had a presence. His blue eyes conveyed depth and security. Clarissa assumed he was a good listener. She was intrigued.

Bryce returned and set her mug on the table. "Do you need sugar or anything?"

"No, thank you. This is perfect." She took a sip and felt the warm liquid move down her throat.

"Well, why don't you tell me what you need?" He took out a pen and small notebook.

"My husband of over twenty years just up and divorced me a few months ago. I opened the door and got served divorce papers. Within three months he had gotten my boys to leave me and move in with him. He bought them cars, games, iPods, whatever, and they went." Clarissa had to pause because of the lump in her throat.

Bryce just watched her intently,

waiting for her to go on.

"Then in the divorce he got full custody, pays me a ridiculous alimony for what he makes, and took the house. I was left with nothing. But that isn't why I called you. I'm not just some upset housewife who thinks her ex has a mistress or something. There is something weird going on." Clarissa reached into her purse and pulled out the receipt. "I found this a while ago. It's the only thing I found in his things that seemed suspicious. The odd thing is the tickets to Idaho. As far as I know he has no family in Idaho. I'm assuming he bought these tickets for him and the boys more than nine months ago and something about that feels wrong. It might be nothing, but my mother's intuition is ringing like mad."

"So do you want me to check out the tickets or find if there is some connection between them? I'm sorry, what's his name?"

"Benjamin Leonard Hadonfield. His parents lived in New York somewhere. That's where I met him anyway. I never met his parents. They were homebound and he didn't seem to want to spend any time with them. I guess that was odd, but you know how things go. In-laws and everything."

Bryce was writing things in the notebook. "He went to school in New York? Do you know where?"

"NYU. He graduated in finance. He started his own company about fifteen years ago. He's done very well for himself and is very well connected. That's why I got screwed at the trial. The judge was a golf buddy."

"Oh, I see." They spent the next few minutes with Bryce asking questions and Clarissa supplying answers. Finally Bryce looked up and said, "Okay, well my fee is per diem and I charge two hundred. Is that going to work?"

Clarissa reached into her purse and handed him an envelope. Inside was six thousand dollars. "That should give you plenty of diem's, right?"

Bryce smiled. "Yes, Clarissa it does. I'm gonna get some work done and get back to you at the end of the week. Will that work for you?"

Clarissa felt a wave of relief. "Yes, thank you. That would be great."

"Listen, Clarissa. If there is anything shady going on with this guy, I'll find it. Don't worry." Bryce winked at her.

"Thank you, Mr. Brightman."

"Call me Bryce." And he stood and left.

FIVE

Bryce called Clarissa at the end of the week and told her that he was on to something and it would take a couple of weeks to get to the bottom of it. Could she meet him in San Francisco two weeks from Thursday? Clarissa was very curious what he was investigating, but stopped herself from asking any questions. She was sure that he would tell her if he thought she needed to know something. They set a time and place and Clarissa wrote it on her calendar.

She kept busy working, doing karate, and hanging out at Becky's house. Becky's husband, Mitchell, was a great guy who should have been a stand-up comedian. Like Becky, he was down to earth, unbelievably smart, and very real. He was tall, with grey hair, a Roman nose, and skinny. A native of San Francisco his family was big, connected, and Italian. He loved to wear t-shirts that had funny sayings on them like 'People say I have ADD but they just don't understand... oh look there's a chicken.' He made Clarissa his pet project and always had a new joke or a funny story to tell her to get her laughing. Of course his job with the Forty-Niner's football team gave him great fodder with all the intrigues of a professional football team. He worked in the front office, and headed up recruitment. He had stories of mothers of potential recruits, their girlfriends, and of course, the wives of the players. It was a plethora of material.

Two weeks eked by and Clarissa fought the temptation to call Bryce and get some of the facts. Finally, she was sitting at the bar at the Clift Hotel waiting for Bryce to get there. She had ordered a martini and was sipping it when he walked up to her.

"Hello, Clarissa. Oh good, you got a drink. I have a table at the restaurant next door." He paid her tab and took her coat. "You hungry?"

"Um, yes. A bit, I guess." She followed him to the hostess stand and they were escorted to their seats.

"I'm sure you are dying to know everything, and I have some interesting stuff to tell you. But if I don't get some food in me I may fall over. Do you mind if we order first?"

"No, not at all. Please." She looked at the menu. The waitress came over and Bryce nodded to Clarissa. After they both ordered the waitress left, and Bryce took out his notebook.

"First off, kudos to your mothers' intuition. Seems you were onto something. I did some poking around in your ex's background and came up with some weird dead ends, so I had some friends from the bureau look into some stuff. Turns out his parents died when he was really young. He was raised by the Hadonfields. But the reason his biological parents died is the start of the story. His original parents started a sort of white supremacist group called, The Truth. It's not like the skinheads you see marching with the swastikas and shaved heads. The principle might be similar, but the way of living the dogma is very different."

"Wait, are you saying that Ben's parents... real parents...were neo-Nazi's?"

"Yes. They were. And even more they were killed in a shootout with one of their own who wanted to change the direction of their group. See Benjamin's original parents, Lois and Harry Jordan, had a new take on an old ideal. They wanted to have their members be upstanding members of society. They would all go to good schools, get top grades, get involved with high finance or politics, and infiltrate all levels of government across America. The whole idea was to change the perspective from the usual group that marches in rallies saying 'Sieg Heil.'"

Their dinner arrived and Bryce dug in. He ate quickly and stopped after a few minutes.

He continued, "They determined that their members would be captains of industry, senators, governors, you know, people of influence and education. And so it began. When his biological parents were killed, Benjamin became the leader and he was raised and also trained in the doctrine by the Hadonfields. That's why he was involved in finance and schmoozed all the big wigs. He was simply following the dogma to become a powerfully connected individual."

Clarissa hadn't moved a muscle or touched her food. She was simply trying to absorb what Bryce was saying. "Wait. I have to take this in."

Bryce finished his dinner and Clarissa finished her martini.

"Now, the people that raised your husband were also part of the organization. They live in Idaho now in a huge mansion your husband bought for them. Of course, it doubles as a nest for their group. Those tickets to Idaho you found were to take your boys to the source of all their power. My guys have heard of this sect. They keep tabs on all these types of groups. You know, Hoover was famous for his surveillance tactics and it's kinda stuck with the bureau."

Clarissa motioned the waitress over and ordered another martini.

"The Truth, as they are called, is all about doing things legally. They don't want violence; they want to rule the world by owning the power and the money. They have been pretty successful so far. Several senators, a few governors, mayors, and lots of Wall Street guys have been connected to the group. But while the agenda seems obvious, there is real activity heating up now that your ex has gotten the boys and is moving to Idaho."

"What?" Clarissa hit the table and the drinks clanked. "He's moving to Idaho with our boys?"

"That's the intel. Seems these members get the rhetoric when they are young and your boys are behind the curve. Your ex is gonna take them in for some intensive training. This is big for the group and there are rumblings that some sort of larger scale action might take place in the near future."

The waitress arrived with Clarissa's martini. Immediately she removed the olives and gulped it down. "I can't believe this. I have to tell my boys. They can't know about this."

Bryce paused.

"What? Is there more?" Clarissa was horrified to hear anything else.

"Well, the FBI is very interested in catching your ex. They are nervous about his agenda, and would like to take this whole group down. But doing that is hard when technically he hasn't broken any laws."

"I don't care about his cult. I care about the boys." Clarissa leaned forward. "I need to get my boys away from him."

"Technically they aren't a cult because it isn't religion based. But...." Bryce nodded in agreement. "We can do that. Get your boys back, but I have to ask you for some help."

Clarissa was still stunned from Bryce's revelation. She looked around the restaurant and saw a table with two men dressed in black suits, one of who was looking at her and was obviously not there for the ambiance. They seemed odd and were not being terribly unobtrusive about staring.

Clarissa leaned towards Bryce and whispered, "Bryce, I think those two men over there are watching us."

"Where are they?" Bryce didn't even react.

Clarissa tried not to nod her head in their direction and spoke while trying not to move her lips. "They are behind you to your right by the wall. Big guys. Both in black suits."

Bryce stood and excused himself. "Wait here, I'll be right back."

He walked out of the restaurant towards the bathroom and Clarissa watched as one man at the table got up to follow him. She was trying not to stare, but it was hard not to. She opened her purse and put on some lipstick, then looked up to see that the other man was gone as well. Slowly, she scanned the whole room, but didn't see him.

A moment later, Bryce was back. He didn't sit down but took her arm while lifting her out of her chair. "Get your purse and let's go."

Clarissa stood, "Wait, where are we going? What about the bill?"

"I got it already. Come on." His voice was even and yet Clarissa could feel the intensity in the words. He pulled her through the bar area which was filled with people. She was jostled as he made his way to the bar and pushed through a black door she hadn't even seen, to another door that led them into the kitchen. The stark white combined with the bright lights hurt her eyes. Ten workers looked up at her and watched as Bryce pulled her quickly through another door which led outside. They were in an alley next to the hotel and Clarissa turned towards the busy street hoping they were going to make a run for it, or at least find anonymity on the street. But instead

Bryce stopped. "Damn it."

Clarissa looked and saw a man in a suit coming towards them and reaching into his coat. She felt a tremor go through her and she thought, *he couldn't have a gun, could he*? A second later she had her answer when he pulled out a gun and pointed it at them.

Bryce opened the door they had just exited from and again pulled Clarissa by the arm. She stumbled, her eyes fixated on the man running with a gun aimed at her.

Bryce yelled at her. "Clarissa, you gotta move."

She went back in the doorway with him and he opened a door she hadn't noticed the first time they'd run through. He pushed her inside, opened the door to the kitchen wide, and then stepped into the closet with her pulling the door shut. His breathing was heavy as Clarissa heard the door they had just come through open with a squeak. Clarissa could just see part of the man's head through the crack in the closet door. She felt Bryce still holding her arm tightly. Clarissa was trying not to pant and hoped that her heartbeat wasn't as loud as it was in her ears. She watched the man go through the kitchen door and it shut behind him. Immediately, Bryce pushed the closet door open. He never let go of her arm as he opened the door to the outside and drug her down the alley to still another door. He used a card key to open it, and they slipped inside. They were on the back stairs of the hotel. Bryce motioned Clarissa to start walking up. At the sixth floor he stepped in front of her and opened the stairway door. He paused as he looked out into the hall. He walked to the first door on the left, used his card key, and the door opened.

Once inside he left her in the entrance hall as he went to check the entire room, including under the bed. He pulled a device from his pocket, turned a switch, and began another sweep of the room. He put his finger to his lips. In a minute, he had been through the whole room again and switched off the device. "Sorry for that."

Clarissa sat on the bed. "What exactly was that? Who were those guys? Why do they have guns? And how did you know about the back door? And when did you get this room?"

Bryce sat in the chair across from her. He took a deep breath and then said.

"Okay, the guys in the restaurant are with The Truth. Well actually, with the SF Police, but technically, with The Truth. I knocked one out in the bathroom, and the other got held up by hotel security because they saw his gun. Hang on." He grabbed the water off the credenza and took a long sip. "I already scoped this place before you got here. And I did work in San Francisco, so I know the staff here and they know me."

Clarissa was still reeling from the 'I'm a spy' exit she just made from the restaurant. "The guys that were watching us work for Ben? The guy with the gun, would he have shot us?"

Bryce never blinked. "Yes."

"He works for Ben?"

"Yes."

"So now he knows that I know what's going on."

Bryce nodded.

"Will Ben hurt me?"

"Probably not. At least not right now. He's gonna wait and see what you do."

Clarissa shook her head. "Probably not? That's not very reassuring."

Bryce looked at the floor. "Sorry, being blunt is kinda my M.O."

Clarissa thought a moment and then asked softly, "What about the boys? He won't hurt the boys?"

"No, they're vital to his organization. He needs to get to them. He plans to indoctrinate them so that they can take his place one day. That's how it's done."

"Oh, my God. My boys would never...." Clarissa trailed off not sure about Jeremy because he wanted his father's attention so much. But Sean? She had a hard time believing he could be part of that.

"Clarissa, I gotta ask if you'd be willing to meet with an agent regarding all this."

"No. I don't want to get involved with that. I also don't want to give Ben any more ammunition to do something to the boys. I just want to get my sons out of this safe. Can you help me with that?"

Bryce stood up and moved across the room. He was thinking. "I know some guys that specialize in getting kids from cults. They may be able to handle this. But it will cost you. Do you have funds to pay for that?"

"How much are we talking about?"

"It will probably be about ten grand.

Do you have that kind of money?"

"Yes. I do. Set it up, Bryce. Please."

"I will. It might take some time because these guys aren't local. In the meantime, you cannot talk to the boys about this. You can't talk to anyone about this. And tomorrow you and I are gonna start training." Bryce clapped his hands together. "Right. I don't want you to go home until you are able to protect yourself. You have a gun?"

"No. I don't know how to use a gun."

"You will."

SIX

Clarissa slept fitfully in the hotel room. First, because she didn't have any of her stuff, so she couldn't wash her face or put her pajamas on. Bryce had left a tooth brush and sweats in the bathroom for her, but it still was odd to be there. And second, because every time she closed her eyes she saw the guy pointing his gun at her.

Lying in bed, she thought about her boys and was truly astonished that this crazy man was their father. He had been her husband. She had spent years being intimate with him, loving him, and it was incredulous to her that she didn't really know who he was. How had she never suspected anything? How had he kept it so completely secret? All these questions made sleeping peacefully out of the question. Finally, around four a.m. she got up and called Becky.

"Hey, I'm sorry. Did I wake you? I know its market day."

Becky yawned. "No, you didn't wake me. I'm just filling my thermos. Where are you?"

"In San Francisco at a hotel."

"Wait...didn't you have dinner with that detective guy last night? You didn't...?"

"No. I didn't. Jeez, Becky. I'm not a slut."

"No. I didn't mean that, but let's be real it's been a while. And you know its all kinda Maltese Falcon and Humphrey Bogart."

"It was nothing like Humphrey Bogart. It was scary as shit. Although, he is handsome." Clarissa paused after saying this out loud.

"Handsome, huh? How handsome? Gerard Butler hot or William H. Macy cute?"

"Um, probably closer to Gerard Butler, although not quite that studly. He has black hair, blue eyes, and a good face. You know clean cut but strong. There is this whole safety thing about him that feels good given my life right now. But that's not what I called about. You're not gonna believe what happened last night?"

"What? Tell me."

Clarissa began the escapade of leaving the restaurant through back rooms, guns, and side alleys when she heard a knock on the door. "Hang on, Becky. Someone is knocking on the door. What time is it?"

"It's four-thirty. That's early for someone to be knocking on the door. Take the phone with you. I can call the police if I need to."

Clarissa did feel her heart pounding even though she wasn't sure she was in danger. She walked to the door and looked through the peep hole. Bryce was standing there. "Becky, it's Bryce. I'll call you later when I get home. Whenever that is."

"Okay. But I'm gonna put a trace out on you if I don't hear from you at least once a day. Tell me when you are coming back, okay. Love you, kiddo." The phone went dead.

"Bye." Clarissa said to dead air. There

was another knock. "Just a minute."

Bryce was inside the door in only a second. "Hey, sorry to come early but it seems you're already up. Were you talking on the phone?" He took the phone away from her. "Let me see that." He pried the back off and stared.

"What are you doing?"

"They're probably monitoring you with the phone's GPS. I'd say toss the phone but we don't want them knowing how much we know. How much did you say just now?"

"I just told Becky what happened last night and then you got here. I didn't get a chance to tell her everything about Ben yet." Clarissa paused. "You think my phone is bugged? Is that what you're saying?"

"Yes. The less they think you know, the better it is for you. I came early to get a good start today. I have a lot to teach you and not a lot of time to do it." He looked around the room. "Are you ready to go?"

"Yes. Let me just get my things." Clarissa moved into the bathroom and found the plastic laundry bag to carry her things in. She double checked the room and walked to Bryce. "Okay. I'm ready."

"You hungry?"

Clarissa hadn't really thought about it but realized she hadn't had any dinner last night and now she was famished. "Yes, actually I'm starving."

Bryce nodded. "We'll stop and pick up some stuff before heading to my place."

"Your place?" Clarissa knew it sounded kinda juvenile. It wasn't like she thought he was going to ravage her. But it did strike a chord that made her want to laugh.

Bryce opened the door and motioned her through. He paused at the stairway and opened the door checking to see if anyone was in there. "Come on."

Clarissa felt her heart again beating quickly, "Should I be worried?"

Bryce looked right at her, "Yes, you should be worried."

Clarissa followed him closely down the stairs and they exited in the same alleyway from last night. She saw a black Ford truck parked in front of them. Bryce walked towards the truck and unlocked the doors. Clarissa pulled herself into the high cab and settled into the seat. She liked the feeling of being in a truck because she could see things and it felt heavy and safe. Bryce started the engine and they headed backwards down the alley. He maneuvered quite well through the traffic as they headed west towards the ocean. Bryce made his way to the Marina district in a very roundabout way, pulled into a garage Clarissa thought the truck would never fit into, and closed the door behind him.

"Okay, we're here."

"I thought we had to go to the store." Clarissa reminded him.

"It's right next door. I'll go after I get you inside."

They exited the truck with not much room to spare. Clarissa had to turn sideways to make it to the door to the apartment.

Bryce stated the obvious. "Careful, these stairs are small and steep."

The incredibly narrow stairs led to a landing. At the top was a door Bryce opened. The apartment seemed good sized and had the slight tinge of the bay breezes blowing through it for years making it smell musty. The foyer was large with hardwood floors. To the right was a family room with a big leather couch and recliner facing a wall with a fireplace. Over the fireplace was a huge big screen television. There was a big window showing part of the apartment across the street, a small view of the water, and part of the Golden Gate Bridge. The walls were painted a deep tan and it was sparse, but clean.

"This is a nice place, Bryce. Can I look around?"

"Sure." Bryce turned to the left into a door way off the foyer which must have been the kitchen. The swinging door creaked as he entered. "I'm gonna make us some coffee and then I'll go down to the store and get us some things for breakfast. Do you like eggs and bacon?"

"Yes, that's fine. Do you want me to go with you?" Clarissa was moving down the hall towards the rest of the apartment.

"No, you stay here. I'm gonna put a video in I want you to watch, okay?"

Clarissa opened doors off the hallway and found his bedroom, a den, and an exercise room. "Okay."

She headed back down the hall to the kitchen. She pushed through another swinging door into a bright kitchen with stainless steel appliances. It was painted beige which made the dark wood cabinets look nice. There was a big round table that looked like an antique. The chairs were mismatched but of good quality. Behind the table was a set of French doors leading to a patio. Clarissa walked to the doors and pushed them open. The patio was brick with grass growing through the cracks. There was a rock retaining wall with roses, plants, and some ivy trailing up the fence. The plants looked wild and as if they were navigating their way out of the garden via the fence. A white metal table and chairs were on one side and a barbeque sat on the other side of the patio. It wasn't very big but it was well appointed and she was surprised that the garden was thriving with no weeds. She sat down for a moment and felt the tired take hold.

The smell of coffee brought her back to hunger. Bryce wasn't in the kitchen so she pushed through the swinging door back to the family room. He was working with a remote and swearing under his breath trying to get the video to work.

"What do you want me to watch?"

"It's a training video from the bureau. It's about hand-to-hand combat. Specifically, how to get away from someone when they attack you. I want you to get familiar and then I will show you how to do it real time, okay?"

"Sure." Clarissa sat on the couch. It was soft and smelled like a new car.

"It's going to start in a second and I'm gonna run downstairs. I'll be back in a minute. Do not call anyone and do not answer the door. I have a key. I'll let myself in. But do not call anyone or they will know where I live and I'd prefer they didn't know that."

"I understand. I'll just watch the video." The film had started with a very clean cut, short-haired man talking about the specifics of hand-to-hand combat.

Bryce left and Clarissa watched the different defensive maneuvers being shown. She was pretty sure she was going to have a hard time learning a lot of them since they were intense. But she also noted that a lot of her karate experience was at play in these techniques. The video was half done when the front door opened and Bryce came through with bags of groceries.

Clarissa jumped off the couch. "Here, let me help you."

"It's okay. I got it." He headed into

the kitchen and Clarissa followed. "How do you like your eggs?"

"Um, it doesn't matter. How were you planning on cooking them?"

"Thought I'd do scrambled." Bryce moved around the kitchen putting things away.

"That's a lot of stuff for just breakfast."

"Well, we're going to be here for a few days while I train you."

"Days?" Clarissa was surprised. "Um, I don't have any clothes or any of my stuff."

"I have sweats you can wear. What stuff do you need?" He looked at her.

Clarissa looked at him with what her sons used to call her 'laser-beams-of-death' stare.

It worked on Bryce too as he reddened. "Oh, you need your make up and stuff. Clarissa, I get this is hard, but I really don't want you going back to your place without some knowledge of how to get out of a bad situation. These guys your ex is mixed up with are not pansies. They will not hesitate to kill you if they need to. Do you get that?"

"Not really until you just said it. They would kill me?" Clarissa felt herself get cold and her head began to swim. "I think I need to sit down."

"If you get in the way, if you make a stink, if you cause problems, then they will kill you. Now do you understand what you're up against? You have to live differently from here on out. You can't tell everyone what you're doing, thinking…it's time to play things very close to the vest."

As she sat at the table Clarissa felt tears on her cheeks. "My boys. He won't hurt my boys will he?"

"No, they're safe because he needs them. But I'm sure he's worried about you getting to your boys. I would imagine he has them pretty well covered. So don't go sneaking around their school or anything like that. When the time is right, we'll get them back."

Now Clarissa was sobbing. "I'm scared, Bryce."

Bryce walked to her, lifted her to him, and held her. She released and let the tears flow. He held her until her sobs got softer. Then he pulled away and looked in her eyes. "Clarissa, we'll get your boys. I promise."

Clarissa looked up into his eyes and believed him. She also felt safe. It was nice to have that feeling again since she'd been existing in a place where she was only reactionary. While she was unsure what was going to happen, she was confident that here she was protected. But she wasn't worried about herself, just her boys. "Bryce, teach me everything and teach me quick."

"Absolutely. Let's get some food in us and then we'll get started."

An hour later they were in Bryce's exercise room. A punching bag hung on a chain from the ceiling, weights littered the floor, and a mat was spread out on one side of the room. Clarissa was wearing a pair of Bryce's shorts using one of his ties to keep them up. She had an FBI t-shirt tucked into the shorts. She had her hands wrapped with tape and was striking the punching bag. Bryce kept telling her to hit harder and she was getting frustrated since she was hitting as hard as she could.

Bryce reached up and removed the bag and pushed everything else out of the way. "Let's try some practical work." He pulled the mat to the center of the room and stepped towards her.

Clarissa nodded, breathing heavily. "Can I get some water first?"

"No, not right now. I'm going to come at you. What are you going to do?"

Clarissa reacted as she had learned at the dojo. She moved in to Bryce's attack and sent the heel of her palm towards Bryce's nose, stopping just in time.

"Good. The karate is going to help you. But you have to know more. Turn around."

For another two hours Bryce attacked her from every direction and Clarissa fought him off. He taught her some new maneuvers and she picked them up pretty quickly, although she was slowing down. The light was fading in the bedroom when Bryce told her to go take a shower and he would make dinner. By the time she had soaked under the hot water trying to get the stiffness from her muscles, dried her hair, and put on the clean sweats he left for her she could smell something good coming from the kitchen.

"Hey, you feel better?" Bryce was just taking some bread from the oven. It looked brown and delicious and Clarissa realized how hungry she was.

"Yes, a shower does a world of good. My gosh, it smells wonderful."

"Just some steak and potatoes. A typical man's meal."

They sat down at the table and Bryce motioned towards her wine glass. "You want some?"

"Yes, please fill it up." Clarissa blushed and looked at him. "Sorry, that didn't sound very good."

"No, it's okay. I get it." He filled up her glass and set the bottle on the table.

Clarissa motioned towards the glass. "You don't drink?"

"No. Not anymore. I got a little too dependent on alcohol. I've been clean for four years. But it doesn't bother me if you drink."

"Is that why you left the FBI?" Clarissa put her fork down and waited for the answer.

"No." He nodded at her plate. "Good?"

"Yes, it's amazing. Thank you." Clarissa felt the evasion and decided it might not be a good idea to press the subject of Bryce's past. They finished their meal sticking with small talk. When they were done, Clarissa insisted on doing the dishes. He went to take a shower and she scrubbed the plates, pans, and glasses thinking about her sons.

"Clarissa?" Bryce entered the kitchen

and she jumped. "Sorry, I didn't mean to scare you."

"Oh, it's okay. I was just lost in thought." She put the last dish in the cupboard and poured some more wine. "So what now?"

"Well, I think you should get some sleep. You can have my room. I changed the sheets."

"I can't take your bedroom. I'm okay on the couch."

"No, you need to get a good night's sleep. It's important you be at your best. You need all your wits about you."

"Bryce?" Clarissa was gonna ask the big question. "What am I gonna do? What's the plan?"

Bryce sighed. "The plan is to get you ready to take care of yourself no matter the circumstances. I want you to keep taking your karate classes. I've filled Dan in on what I want him to teach you. Then I'm going to find out more about your ex and his game plan. I will contact the people I know and we'll get your sons back. Okay?"

"That sounds simple." Clarissa finished her wine with a big gulp. "I never would have thought in a million years that this is where I would find myself."

Bryce nodded. "Nobody ever does."

SEVEN

Three days later Clarissa was prepared enough, in Bryce's eyes, to go home. She was nervous, but still felt fairly certain she could defend herself if she needed to. Between her karate and what Bryce had been drilling into her she was feeling pretty strong. She also felt sure that she needed to be more aware of what was happening. This threat was real and even more, her boys were direct targets.

Bryce had told her she needed to make sure she was continuously aware and gave her a list of things she had to do if he was going to let her go back to the cottage. It was imperative she went home since living in sweats two sizes too big and having no privacy was driving her nuts. Bryce was an interesting man, but feelings and emotions were not his forte and she wasn't sure what she felt about him. He was handsome and exciting, but there was a reserve that she couldn't break through and that is why she needed to get away from him.

Arriving back at the cottage she was wary and kept her eyes peeled. At the door she checked to make sure it was still locked. She looked at the door jam and the windows making sure they didn't look like they had been tampered with. Walking through the door she held her breath and listened. No sound came back to her so she made her way to the kitchen and she set her purse down with the laundry bag from the hotel. She took the bug locater out of her purse and turned it on. Bryce had told her to sweep the cottage so she could know what he was saying was real.

Clarissa moved through the kitchen waving it over the counters and it began softly beeping. Over the stove in the vent she located the first bug. She left it where it was and kept moving. Ending in the bedroom she had found six bugs throughout the cottage.

The last one was behind her headboard. She sat on the bed and felt warm tears running down her face. Damn it. She didn't want this all to be real. She wanted her sons back and life to be not necessarily the same, but better than it was right now. Clarissa didn't want the fear that was lodged in her chest anymore. The phone rang making her jump and shaking her out of her reverie.

Clarissa reached for the phone by the bed checking herself to remember the bug and not let her guard down. "Hello."

"Hi hon, you home now?" Becky was on the other end.

"Yes, I just walked in."

"How was it?"

"Good trip. I had a good time. It was nice to get away." Clarissa had already called Becky from a secure location filling her in on everything including the fact that her parent's cottage was bugged. Becky had thought they should call the police. But Clarissa had told her that Bryce was connected with the FBI and that he was better than the police since she couldn't be sure of their allegiance.

"You wanna come for dinner tonight? Oh, and my parents let me know they extended their trip. They plan to be gone another few weeks, are you okay with that?

"That's fine. And no, I'm beat and going to stay in tonight. I'll see you tomorrow at work."

"Sure thing. Take it easy and rest. See you tomorrow, kiddo."

After Clarissa hung up she filled up the big white bathtub as hot as she could and soaked for an hour easing the pain of her sore muscles and bruised body. Then she made a quick dinner and sat to catch up with her shows on TiVo. About one a.m. she settled in her bed and lay there blinking at the ceiling. Thoughts raced and she tried breathing slowly to calm her brain and somewhere mid-breath she finally fell asleep. She dreamt that she and Bryce were fighting off a dragon. It was getting smoky because the dragon was breathing fire and she felt the smoke suffocating her as she began to cough. The coughing woke her up and she sat up in bed. She had left the light on in the bathroom with the door closed to keep some brightness in the room. Getting up she looked around and listened; only silence responded.

Clarissa went through the next week following the rules that Bryce had put into place. No personal calls on her cell or home phone. If she did phone anyone she couldn't tell them anything, and had to keep the calls short. She worked at Floration, ate at Becky's house, and trained with Dan. Every day she checked the whole house to make sure nothing was out of place before eating, watching television, or going to bed. Every night she had nightmares. She got adept at determining if a sound in the night was something she should respond to or ignore.

Per Bryce's instructions she had put mace in several places throughout the house that she could easily get to and she had a knife under her mattress. Bryce had taught her how to get out of a room and she played the scenario over and over in her mind. She was always on alert and ready to react. Dan had been drilling self-defense moves per Bryce's instructions. She was becoming lean and strong. And while she should be nervous, instead she felt a calm that indicated she was focused on self-preservation.

Every day she went to a phone booth and called her boys. They never answered her calls and twice she found their numbers had been disconnected. Bryce's contacts were always able to find their new numbers and she kept up the twice daily calls leaving her love on their voicemail. She never wanted them to think that she had forgotten them.

Yesterday she had met with Bryce but first had to evade someone tailing her. She gave him the money he needed to get her boys back. She was proud that she hadn't been scared, merely determined. She was sure that she had crossed a line from the Clarissa she had used to be. This Clarissa was not as naive or gullible as the old one. This Clarissa paid attention and listened to everything. This Clarissa was prepared and thought ahead every moment to be sure to be ready if she needed to defend herself.

Tonight she had drunk a glass of wine, even though Bryce had recommended she not drink before bed so her reflexes would be up to par. But she was restless and needed to sleep. She felt the nightmare descending with the presence of the dragon once again as she dipped into sleep. This night she moved towards the threat with a sword in her hand. The dragon sent fire out to burn her and the smoke that was left behind kept her vision impaired. She began to cough in her dream and found she awoke hacking and having trouble catching her breath. She tried to move from the cobwebby feeling of the dream, clearing her throat, and listening. Something was wrong. Clarissa felt unusual. Turning towards the bathroom door she let her eyes adjust to the sliver of light coming from the door. When her eyes focused, she sat up.

Bringing her feet to the floor she paused and saw a shadow out of the corner of her eye. Instantly her heart began to pound and she could feel her blood moving faster in her veins. *Oh my God, someone is in here,* she thought while forcing herself to breathe slower and keep her wits. All the moves Bryce taught her were running through her brain. Once she quieted her mind the training kicked in and she figured surprise was her best bet. She stood up, sliding her feet into her slippers so she had traction if she needed to fight someone.

Moving towards her bathroom she kept herself ready for an attack from behind. As she opened the door to the bathroom the light flowed into the room and she saw someone standing in the corner. Stepping into the bathroom she grabbed the mace she had placed behind the planter earlier in the week and palmed it in her hand. Then she turned.

"I see you there." She was standing in the doorway and could see the shadow but not the face. "What do you want? Who are you?"

"It's me, Clarissa."

Clarissa instantly recognized his voice. "Ben?"

"Yes."

"What are you doing in my house? How did you get in?" Clarissa was careful not to let on she knew anything in the tone of her voice.

"I think you know why I'm here." He stepped towards her and she could see his face. It was hard and cold and she marveled that she had ever loved this man.

"I do?"

"Nosey as always, aren't you?"

Clarissa heard a click of a gun. She stepped forward and adjusted the mace in her hand. "What do you mean?" Playing dumb felt like the right thing to do and Bryce had drilled into her mind to trust her instincts.

"I know you know who I am. I also know that you have gotten some help. There isn't much I don't know. My question for you is what are you going to do about it? See, while I know you think you can outsmart me or out maneuver me, you can't. I know everything you do. I know you call the boys every day, twice a day."

"Really, how do you know all this? Are you following me?"

"I have my ways. Now, I'm only here because we used to be married and I was fairly certain that you would believe me when I told you that if you don't let things alone and go about your life it's going to get very bad for you." He stepped closer to Clarissa and she moved one foot back to shift her weight while subduing her outrage.

"Really? You think I'm afraid of you?"

"You should be."

"Oh, I see. I should be afraid of the biggest bully I have ever met?" Clarissa smiled. "You know what? I'm not afraid of you."

"My dear Clarissa, this is a courtesy. Next time someone comes it will not be to talk. Do you understand?" He sneered and pulled the gun from his pocket. He turned it in his hand and pointed it at her. "This is your warning to back off. Stay out of my business and don't make me send someone to kill you."

Clarissa took another step towards him so now she was only inches away from his face. "If you think that I am going to let you take my children away from me then you don't have a clue who I am. If you think I am going to roll over and let you do whatever you want with them then you have gravely underestimated my strength, determination, and will. You, Ben, are the one that needs to be worried. I will never abandon my boys." Clarissa was glaring at him. "Never." She brought her hand up in a quick motion and sprayed mace right into his face.

Ben yelled and grabbed his eyes. Clarissa sprayed more mace and shoved him away. He stumbled and fell, still clutching his eyes. She grabbed the bag she had set by the door, her car keys, and pulled her bedroom door shut. Taking a screwdriver from the cabinet outside her bedroom she unscrewed the screws pulling the door handle off the door then jammed the screwdriver sideways into the mechanism.

Clarissa grabbed the bag and her purse and ran out the front door. Ben's black sedan was parked behind her car. She got into hers, started the engine, put her seat belt on, and then threw her car into reverse. She rammed into Ben's car pushing it into the hedges and then moved into drive, made a quick turn, and peeled out down the driveway. As she did she found the disposable phone in her purse and pushed one. The sound of the ring was challenged by the sound of her blood coursing through her body.

Bryce's voice came groggily on the line. "Hello."

"It's on."

"They made contact?"

"Just now. It was Ben himself. I maced him, locked him in my bedroom, and took off."

"Okay, go where we said. I'll meet you there in an hour."

"See you then."

EIGHT

The door to the motel creaked as Clarissa pushed it open. She could smell the mustiness of unuse, the ocean, and the need for new...everything. Frowning, she turned the light on, shut the door, and set her bag on the bed. Looking around she realized her first impression was dead on. This room was old, faded, and needed a large bucket of Lysol to clean away the dinginess. She remembered what that news report had said about bedspreads and what they found using a black light and she shivered and removed her bag from the bed.

What the hell was Bryce thinking,

Clarissa wondered to herself as she heard a knock on the door. There was a pause then three more knocks. She counted to five and three more knocks occurred and she sighed and unlocked the door. Bryce was standing there and turned to look over his shoulder as he stepped into the room.

"You okay?" He closed the door and looked intently at her.

Clarissa paused, distracted by the look in Bryce's eyes and the proximity to him. "Um, yes. I'm okay. I was scared but I managed to forget about that when I saw this room."

Bryce looked around and chuckled. "Sorry about this." He nodded towards the bed. "It's the most remote place I know of. Now that this game is on you can stay with me. But we'll leave your car here. Do you think you were followed? And did you park it in the back?"

"No. I took extreme precautions even heading the opposite direction before changing up and heading back this way. No one followed me. And yes, I did park it back there."

Bryce nodded. "You covered it?"

"Yes. Will it be alright here?"

"I'll send someone to pick it up and drop it off at Becky's house. Ready to go? Unless you'd rather stay here?" Bryce winked at her.

Clarissa laughed. "No, Bryce. I'd rather stay outside in a tent than in here. Where did you find this place?"

"A guy I know used this place as a drop. It was what popped into my mind. I always trust those instincts. So let me get your bag and we'll go. The car is a blue sedan looking thing and is parked to the right. Go get it and drive up to the driveway and I'll get in. Okay?" He handed her the keys.

Clarissa went to take her bag. "No, I'll get that; you just go get the car." Bryce opened the door slowly and looked both ways. "Go now."

Clarissa walked down the hallway looking into the windows. All the curtains were drawn and no one seemed to be stirring behind them. The parking lot only had two cars so she assumed this wasn't a hot location for overnight guests. Turning the corner she saw the blue sedan parked by some trees. She checked the back seats before getting in and then slid behind the steering wheel. The car was huge and the wheel moved slowly to turn the enormous car. She thought she must look ridiculous since you couldn't see all of her head over the headrest. When she reached the driveway she paused and Bryce slid into the front seat and told her to drive.

They spent over an hour getting to his house. Multiple times he told her to turn down streets and stop and they would duck down and wait. At one point they pulled into a driveway and ducked down spending ten minutes in silence. Finally, he told her to pull into a car lot and park in the garage. As they emerged from the car, a young kid whose pants hung down in the fashion that Clarissa would never let her boys wear, took the keys that Bryce threw to him.

"Yo, what's up with the grandpa car?"

"Hey, Joseph. It's my Nana's. Park it for me will ya?"

"Sure, dude. See ya later."

Clarissa couldn't suppress a smile. "That's your grandma's car? Really?"

Bryce looked at her and winked. "No, my grandma is dead. But he doesn't need to know that."

They made their way cautiously to Bryce's apartment going down alleys and stopping often so Bryce could make sure they weren't being followed. They finally stopped at a fence and Bryce got down and motioned for Clarissa to step onto his hands so he could lift her over the fence. Amazingly, she managed to get over the fence and landed lightly. All the training was doing its job and she felt sorta like a ninja. Once inside he put her suitcase in his room and joined her back in the kitchen. She had a glass of wine already poured. "So, what's next?"

"Here, I want to give you this." He handed her a box.

"What's this?" Clarissa opened the box and saw a gold necklace with a locket. "Oh, Bryce, this is beautiful." She felt kind of embarrassed wondering if he was thinking there was something between the two of them.

"It's a tracking device and I want you to wear it all the time."

She tried to cover up her first thoughts before Bryce could read her disappointment. "Oh, tracking device, of course. Wow, they make them look really nice don't they."

"We're meeting with a colleague of mine from the job. He has some insight into what we are looking at with Ben and why he's moving now. There must be a reason that he's making the move with the boys, but we don't know what it is. So we're gonna have to use some intelligence to figure out what our next step is going to be. Right now get some sleep and we can talk about this more tomorrow."

Clarissa drank the rest of her wine and nodded at Bryce. She realized that she was completely exhausted and that all the running today had taken its toll on her. "Okay, I'll see you tomorrow morning."

The next morning she went to the kitchen expecting to see Bryce and instead an older man with grey hair was sitting at the table. Clarissa backed up, took Bryce's taser from the shelf, and then opened the door while pointing the gun at the man. "Who are you? Where is Bryce?"

"Hi, you must be Clarissa. I'm Doug. I worked with Bryce at the agency." He started to go into his pocket for something. "Here are my creden…."

Clarissa reacted as he got up from the table and moved toward her, she pulled the trigger and the taser exploded. He instantly went down and lay shaking on the floor.

Clarissa screamed when she heard the front door open, dropped the taser, and ran out the back door to the patio. She was half way over the fence when she heard Bryce's voice.

"What the heck are you doing? What happened to Doug? Did you taze him?"

Clarissa's leg was halfway over the fence and she was dangling over both sides. "Um, yes. Is he really from the FBI? I'm sorry, I just kinda reacted." She tried to pull her leg back over and heard Bryce laughing.

She jumped back down while he laughed so hard he was bending over. "Damn, what did Doug do before you got him?"

"Well, he tried to talk to me but I didn't believe him. I mean, he could have been anyone. I'm sorry. Is he gonna be okay?" Clarissa came through the door still tentative and unsure what the FBI agent was going to do to her once he got his bearings.

Doug was sitting on the floor cursing under his breath. When Clarissa entered the room he tried to stand up. "What the hell…."

"I'm so sorry, Doug. It is, Doug, right? Bryce has me on high alert and you were just sitting in the room and I don't know…I mean I've been dealing with a lot and I...I panicked. I'm so sorry. Are you alright?" Clarissa took a step toward him to help him up.

Doug slowly got to his feet, gave her a dirty look, and sat down at the table again. "Do you want to see my credentials now?"

Bryce was roaring with laughter and trying to catch a breath. "Damn Doug, you must have really scared her."

"Shut up, Bryce. Can I get some coffee?"

Clarissa got a cup, filled it and handed it to him. "Cream or sugar?"

"No, black is fine. Ms. Hadonfield, I have to talk to you about your ex-husband. Did you know what he is involved in?"

"No. I had absolutely no idea until after he took the boys and I hired Bryce. Everything that happened this last year has been a shock. But the worst is that I can't see my boys and don't know if they are alright."

"They are fine. Both of them are continuing their schooling. Your elder son has been driving and he is doing quite well, even with the kind of car he has access to. Your ex has been doing a lot of travel and he takes the boys with him. They rarely leave his side and when they are gone at school someone tails them. They are precious cargo to him."

"Well, that's odd given the fact that he didn't pay much attention to them when they were small and we were together."

"It's a new regime now. He is ready to move this group to the next level. We surmise that this group's intention is to take control of the United States by procuring the presidency with one of their own. However, we are not sure who they are going to use since their ties are so broad and mainstream that any of a dozen high profile officials could be in their grasp. We are watching everyone we can but we're not sure if we are missing something. I wanted to see if I could glean any information from you regarding your ex-husband's state of mind, who he associated with, and behaviors when you were together. Would you be willing to look at some pictures?"

"Sure." Clarissa winced as he pulled two large stacks out of a briefcase on the floor. "Wow, that's a lot of pictures."

Two hours later her eyes were bleary and she had still a quarter of a stack of pictures to go. Bryce had been moving about the apartment while she turned the pictures and Doug asked her repeatedly if any faces looked familiar. She was almost done when she stopped and looked at the man in the image.

"What? Do you know him?" Doug moved to the edge of his seat. "Does he look like someone your husband knew?"

"Actually, I think I saw him at some event we went to for Ben's office. It was a charity event. Expensive. Everyone there had a lot of money judging by their wives necks. He was there and he and Ben chatted briefly. Or at least I think it was brief since I was returning from the ladies room when they were talking."

Doug took the photo and made some notations on the back.

"Who is he? Do you know him?" Clarissa wanted to know if he was involved with Ben's group.

"Is he an important guy?"

"Yes. He's a Senator."

"Really?" Clarissa sighed. "Is he involved with the group?"

Doug looked up from his briefcase. "Since he was talking to Ben I'm going to surmise he is, although I will have to do some legwork before I can be sure. I'll get back to you." Doug collected all his things as Bryce came into the room.

He looked from Doug to Clarissa. "So, did you find anything?"

Clarissa waited for Doug to speak and when he didn't she said, "I found a picture of a senator that Ben met at a party once. Doug is going to check it out."

Doug had his case and nodded to Bryce. Clarissa could tell it was a secret code to meet him in the hall so they could talk privately. "Doug, it was nice to meet you. I'm going to go to my room for a while. Thank you for your help. So sorry about the stun gun."

"It's okay. And it was a pleasure to meet you too."

Clarissa doubted he really meant that.

NINE

Bryce had left early in the morning leaving Clarissa to pace around the house for the last hour trying to find something to occupy her mind. She found a note on the coffee table taped to a CD case. *Clarissa, you need to watch this.*

Bryce must have left it for her. She opened the case and found the player, amazingly remembering how Bryce had put in the DVD the other day and before she knew it she had sound but no picture. Clarissa went to push another button, but stopped. The voice on the TV was familiar. She cocked her head as if to hear more clearly. Suddenly, she recognized the voice. It was Ben.

Frantically she pushed buttons until the screen whined and an image came on the TV. It was blurry and she had to step back to see anything. It was a room; she could make that much out. It looked like a conference room as there appeared to be several people sitting around the table. The black box in the corner of the image said FBI tape 22. She sat down in the chair and listened. Ben was quiet and others were talking about men she didn't know. She continued listening until she heard Ben speak again. He was forceful and sounded different than she ever had heard him.

It is time to start actively pursuing the individuals that we think have a chance at being considered for the race. We don't want to put forward someone who isn't....

Clarissa turned the volume up but Ben had stopped talking. It sounded like someone else had entered the room. There was movement on the grainy image but discerning anyone's face was impossible. Ben began to speak again.

As I was saying, we need to make sure that there are no issues to thwart our next endeavors. The problem with the last candidate and his unscrupulous sexual appetite shouldn't have been missed. So I want double duty on these three men until we are sure they are above reproach. Is that clear?

Several people began to talk and Ben cut them off.

I don't give a fuck what you think. This is my organization and I will run it in the manner it was built upon. I am not fucking around guys. We will have this seat in the Senate and we will be moving up this ladder in the next couple.....

Clarissa heard a bang, like something falling over, and then the tape went blank. She sat there frozen. She had no idea who that man was other than the fact that he had Ben's voice. It wasn't anyone she knew. A chill ran through her body as she realized this wasn't a joke. Ben was seriously going to take her boys away and she would never see them again. A sob escaped her throat before she had to run to the toilet and vomit.

After she cleaned herself up she put her locket on and left a note on the table for Bryce. She had to see the boys because while she was worried before, she was paralyzed with fear for them now. Doug had said things were progressing quite quickly which meant that Ben could take them before she could rescue them. She had to do what her heart was telling her to do. Clarissa had to see her sons.

An hour and a half later she was parked a block from their school. She had made the taxi driver go through the student parking lot so she could find Jeremy's car and then she had him park so she could watch it from the street. Clarissa had paid him cash up front so he was willing to take all the time she needed. School would be out in five minutes and she made sure to keep an eye out for whoever Ben had tailing the boys. So far she hadn't seen anything unusual until a minute before the bell was to ring when a black SUV pulled into the student parking lot and stopped. She figured that must be the boy's tail. She wasn't stupid enough to try to talk to the boys, but she just had to see them.

The bell rang and teenagers exploded from the building. Clarissa kept her eye focused on Jeremy's car and waited to catch a glimpse of him. She barely breathed as she saw the parking lot thin out as teens squealed out of their spots. Finally, she saw Jeremy and Sean walking together toward the car. Clarissa felt tears come immediately. They both looked taller and older. Jeremy was telling Sean something and Sean laughed and Clarissa felt her heart breaking. The need to hug them was beyond anything she'd ever felt before, but she made herself sit lower in the backseat. Jeremy nodded at the black SUV and got into the car. He pulled out of his spot and the SUV followed. As they drove past her, Clarissa sank further down and the sobs racked her body.

The taxi driver turned around asking, "You alright lady?"

"Yes. Just drive, will you?" Clarissa gave him directions to a pay phone and called Becky at Floration. Becky knew the code and twenty minutes later Clarissa heard her pre-paid cell phone ringing.

"You okay?" Becky didn't hesitate.

"Are you at the pay phone?"

"Yes."

"The same one as before?"

Becky paused. "No, 1 found one three blocks away from the shop. Is that okay? So what happened?"

"I just saw the boys."

"What? How did you see them?"

"I parked down the street from their school."

Becky didn't answer right away and Clarissa could hear the intake of breath. "Honey, are you crazy?"

"Becky, I can't stand it. I haven't seen them in too long. I swear I ache for them. What must they think about me?"

"But sweetie, you told me you call them every night. They know you care."

"That's not enough. They should see me caring for them. They should know what they're involved in. I feel like I've led my sons to slaughter. I have to get them away from him. Becky, I.... "

"What happened? You sound worse. What made you go there?"

Clarissa paused and took a deep breath. "Bryce brought a friend, an agent he knows, to the apartment. He showed me pictures of people to see if I ever saw them with Ben. One of them I'd seen before, but that isn't what freaked me out."

"What freaked you out?"

"The guy left a DVD and I watched it this morning. It was some FBI surveillance tape and you couldn't see anything clearly, but the sound was perfect. I heard Ben talking to the group and I swear on my life, it scared me to my core. He sounded completely...I don't know...evil. I knew it was his voice, but it wasn't anyone I had ever met, or knew. I might have been married to this man, but I never knew him. I slept with a stranger. Oh Becky...."

"Honey, I know this all probably feels like something from the Twilight Zone but you gotta stay tough and know that Bryce is gonna help you. He will get the boys back for you. You gotta take your time, honey. You are up against something bigger than you. Trust that Bryce can do this. You do trust him, right?"

"I've put a lot of faith in him, and yes, I do trust him. I know he's my best shot at rescuing the boys."

"Clarissa, I can't even imagine how you feel right now. It must be horrible finding out your love was so wrongly misplaced. Even if Ben is a creeper, your boys are going to be home and you'll be able to hug them soon. I swear I just feel that, okay?"

Clarissa sighed. "Thanks, Becky. Seriously, you are such a good friend doing the whole cloak and dagger bit every time you call. And as much as I'd like to stay here and talk to you more I'd better get going 'cause Bryce is probably going to kill me for leaving his place. Thanks for listening, Becky."

"Honey, anytime. You hang in there, okay? Have faith. This will work out, I swear it will. I love you, friend."

"I love you too." Clarissa closed the phone. Once she disconnected she felt the loneliness again. She told the taxi driver where to go. Forty-five minutes later she was throwing her leg over the back fence. She jumped quietly to the ground then tip-toed to the kitchen door. Standing in the doorway was an obviously angry Bryce.

Clarissa opened the door. "I'm sorry. I just had to go out for a bit."

"Are you trying to get caught? Do you want Ben to find you and kill you?" Bryce was seething. "This is not a game, Clarissa. You are in very grave danger and taking off like that is not a smart play."

"I know and I'm sorry. But Bryce...."

"Where did you go?"

Clarissa looked down to the floor.

"You did not."

Clarissa looked up slowly and met

Bryce's eyes.

"Tell me you didn't go and see the boys."

"Bryce, I saw the video and I just...I don't know I had to see the boys and I guess make sure they were still okay. Still here."

"Oh my God, you're a fool, you know. Why am I bothering?" He stormed off.

"Bryce...." the words faded as she saw his back retreat into the office and the door slam behind him.

Clarissa busied herself making dinner. She found everything for lasagna and an hour later it was bubbling in the stove making the whole house smell delicious. She sat at the table with a glass of wine thinking about the boys and how they had looked. Bryce walked in to her lost in the reverie and the smell of lasagna.

"Hi." He took a soda from the fridge. "Clarissa, don't think I don't understand how you feel. I do. I have a son too."

Clarissa's head popped up as she looked at him. "You do?"

"Yes, that's part of the reason I took the retirement."

"Are you divorced? And where is he?

Do you see him?"

He smiled at her barrage of questions. "Yes, I'm divorced. We agents don't always make the best husbands. My ex got tired of the secrecy and the lack of emotions, or so she said." Bryce took a long gulp of his drink. "I see my son once a month for a week. Because of my job it's been hard for me to keep him with me in the usual joint custody. So I pick him up and take him away for a week at a time so that we can spend some quality time together."

Clarissa nodded. "So you understand the missing."

"Yes, I do. But I also need you to understand that going to see them puts you in grave danger. We are not dealing with a businessman that is simply worried about money. Ben is planning on taking over the United States and implementing his doctrine through the presidency. And you don't know what his doctrine is, do you?"

"No."

"He's a white supremacist. Unlike the usual skinheads he wants to make his doctrine part of the American public's ideals. This sect is very atypical because while they utilize the skinheads and neo-Nazi's to help facilitate their path, they do not equate themselves with them. They believe they are superior and their doctrine coming from the top will make it valid. Their hope is if the President of the United States says it then the American people will follow. And honestly, they're probably right about that. People tend to be sheep."

"But Bryce, how are we going to get the boys away? They're being followed."

"It does pose a problem to get past them, but I think we can do it with the four of us."

"Four of us? Who...."

"Twin brothers. Their parents joined a cult in the eighties and they were both trapped there from the time they were born. When they were twelve they ran away and managed to get emancipated. They worked their way through the heavyweight boxing circuit and when they became twenty-one they started this business. They are the best at what they do."

"They're heavyweight boxers? Famous ones?"

"Not exactly, but they are known in the sport. They're both remarkably strong. But their forte is their ability to snatch and clean."

"Snatch and clean? What's that?"

"Well, getting the individuals out of the cult is the first step. They are good at figuring out the best place where they can apprehend their marks and then they're unbeatable at cleaning out the rhetoric." The timer on the oven went off and Bryce got up and pulled the lasagna from the oven. "These are the ones you want for a situation like this."

"When are we planning...or are they planning on getting the boys?"

"I'm not sure. They'll let me know when they have figured out the best time. Until then, you have to keep cool and do as I say. Are you willing to do that?"

Clarissa nodded. "Listen, I know I took a risk today, but I couldn't stop myself. I needed to see the boys. I haven't seen or spoken to them in months and I just felt like they were getting too far away. After hearing Ben on that tape I realized that he's nothing like what I thought he was. His voice was cold and harsh and completely malevolent. You know?"

Bryce put a plate of lasagna and salad down for Clarissa. "Yes, I know. But don't take the chance again. Tell me something, how was the layout at the school? Was it somewhere we could consider to get the boys back?"

"The parking lot is in front, so there is access. But they have body guards that arrived right before school let out. So I don't know if it would work."

"Okay, well I'll mention it to the guys. Let's eat. You want something to drink?"

Bryce changed the subject asking Clarissa about her childhood and she forgot a bit about the sadness in her heart. She enjoyed talking to Bryce, but while she would've thought there would be some sort of romantic aspects to their interactions, and Clarissa wasn't sure she would be against that, Bryce had an abrupt way most of the time. He answered questions short and to the point and his emotions rarely showed. He wasn't mean or annoyed, simply a product of his environment. He'd learned to turn off the feelings being in the FBI and Clarissa guessed that's probably what killed his relationship with his wife. There was an aloofness that felt impenetrable and really kinda froze you out. That combined with Clarissa's utter one track mind of getting her boys back made anything else irrelevant.

After dinner they had an early evening. Clarissa re-read the same magazine for the umpteenth time and fell asleep. She awoke to someone shaking her. She opened her eyes a bit to see Bryce looking at her.

"You awake?"

She sat up and rubbed her eyes looking around to get her bearings. "What's going on? Is something wrong?"

"No. Everything's okay. The guys are here and I told them about the school thing and they think it might work. They want to discuss the plan. But...it's two in the morning, you up to it?"

Clarissa was squinting up at Bryce. "Why are they here at two in the morning?"

"Who knows, they are like that. They probably were out and got an idea. I don't know exactly, but they're here, and if you're able, they'd like to go over the plan."

"Give me a minute." Clarissa stumbled into the bathroom and put some water on her face. She could feel her eyes focusing slowly. "Hmm, two o'clock in the morning. Odd."

In the family room sat two of the biggest men Clarissa had ever seen. They were about six feet five inches tall and looked about that broad across. Both of them had shaved heads and arms the size of her thighs. They were sitting on the couch and when she came into the room wearing Bryce's sweatshirt that hung down to her knees, they both stood up and said, "Ma'am."

Clarissa looked at Bryce quizzically. "Um, hello. I'm Clarissa. It's nice to meet you."

"Hello, ma'am." The one with a scar on his cheek moved forward and enveloped her hand into his huge palm. She felt immediately dainty and petite, which of course she wasn't.

"Hello." She turned to the other twin. "I'm Clarissa." She again extended her hand.

"I'm very pleased to make your acquaintance, ma'am." The other twin actually seemed bigger than the former. Again her hand disappeared into the huge grasp of what she hoped was her savior.

Bryce looked at Clarissa and said, "This is Timothy and Tony Minesco."

Both the men nodded at Clarissa and Tony said, "Sorry for the late hour but besides Bryce's safety issues we also sometimes get our best ideas in the middle of the night. Hope that's okay?"

"Sure, I'm just glad you guys are thinking about how to get my boys."

"Well, Bryce mentioned that you had been at the boy's school the other day and we actually had some good ideas. Would you like to sit down?"

TEN

A week later, after more drills than Clarissa cared to think about, she and Bryce sat hunched down in the front seat of Bryce's grandmother's car. Clarissa could feel her body temperature rising and took a napkin from the dash, dabbing at her upper lip and forehead.

"You okay?" Bryce nodded at her.

"Yes, just a little nervous. And it's hot in here. How much longer?"

"About ten minutes." The walkie talkie squawked and Bryce said, "Come again."

The voice was garbled but Clarissa

could tell it was one of the twins. She looked over the sill out the window and saw that the tow truck had moved both of the cars parked next to Jeremy's. Now the twins were sitting in cars parked on either side of Jeremy's car. It was quiet and Clarissa listened for the sound of a truck coming up behind them. The bodyguards should be arriving soon. They usually arrived five minutes before school was out.

"Bryce, you sure this will work?" Clarissa just wanted to hear him say it.

"Yes, I do. Maybe you should just wait here."

Clarissa looked at Bryce and anger flashed. "Why? Don't you think I can handle it?"

Bryce's expression never changed. "Well, it's not that exactly, more that I think when you see them you might become...."

"What? Weak? Cry? Lose it?" Clarissa could tell by Bryce's face it was what he was thinking. "I want the boys to see me. And you might need me to explain what's going on."

Bryce sunk lower in his seat. He spoke into the walkie talkie. "We got shadows."

Clarissa looked over the sill to see the

black SUV pull into the parking lot. Both the twins were now lying down in their front seats so they couldn't be seen. The black SUV pulled into a staff parking space a few cars away. They idled and settled in to wait. The minutes clicked by on the dashboard clock. Finally Clarissa heard the bell ring and her heart started beating faster. "Calm yourself." She said it so softly that Bryce didn't even hear. The last thing she wanted was to prove the concerns he had of her being involved.

Bryce watched the kids leaving the school and every so often looked at the pictures of the boys Clarissa had given him. It was quiet except for the chatter of the kids exiting and the sound of motors starting up.

"I see them." Bryce squawked the walkie talkie two times and then one squawk came back. The twins were ready. Clarissa was looking over the dashboard when Bryce said, "Come on."

They walked quickly towards the parking lot. They didn't want to run and draw undo attention.

Clarissa could see Jeremy and Sean were almost to the doors of their car and the SUV was beginning to back out. That was good because then the bodyguards wouldn't be able to act as quickly. As Clarissa made it to Jeremy's car he and Sean were just opening the door when Sean yelled out, "Mom?"

Clarissa said, "Hi, honey."

Jeremy turned to look and both the twins jumped out of the car. Tony grabbed Sean and Tim tried to grab Jeremy. In an instant Jeremy seemed to figure out what was going on and he jumped in his car even though Tim was grabbing his arm. The SUV stopped, the passenger door opened, and a gigantic guy got out with a gun drawn. He pointed it at Tony and fired. Tony went down and Sean screamed.

Clarissa ran to the front of the car, "Jeremy and Sean, you have to come with me. Your dad is going to take you away. I won't be able to see you and I love you and miss you so much." Sean was staring at her and Jeremy had his door closed and was revving the engine. Clarissa saw Tony lying on the ground, he wasn't moving and his eyes were open. Jeremy pushed the car forward and Clarissa had to jump out of the way. "Jeremy!" Clarissa screamed.

"Sean, get in now." Jeremy yelled at

him.

Sean jumped into the passenger seat and Jeremy pushed the gas. Clarissa saw Sean's wide eyes filled with tears as Jeremy squealed out of the parking lot. The SUV followed closely behind.

"Oh my god, it didn't work." Clarissa fell to the ground. Tim and Bryce were feeling Tony's neck for a pulse. Tim started pushing on his chest but Bryce touched his shoulder and shook his head. Tim, the huge man that he was, seemed to be no smaller than a child as he kneeled next to his brother.

"Tim, I'm so sorry. Oh God, how did this get so messed up?" Clarissa could feel the hot tears on her face and saw Sean's face etched in her mind. "Bryce, what are we going to do now?"

Bryce walked to Clarissa and took her arm. He didn't speak but walked her to his car and put her in. Then he went back to the parking lot. By now all the remaining kids were standing around trying to get a look at the guy lying on the ground. A few were trying to stand on cars to take pictures with their phones. Tim grabbed Tony's body under the arms and Bryce opened the back door. They slid Tony onto the seat and Bryce nodded at Tim. In mere moments and with no words, Tim drove his dead twin off the campus of the high school. Bryce returned to the car.

"What are we going to do now?" Clarissa asked with eerie calm staring straight ahead.

"Well, obviously this didn't go well. We wanted surprise on our side. And now we've lost the twins. On top of which, now Ben knows we're on the move. So for now we have to go low profile. We'll rethink the plan and see what to do next. Okay?" Bryce looked at Clarissa. "I'm sorry. I really am."

Clarissa began to sob. "Poor Tony. What's Tim going to do?"

"He'll take care of it his own way. For now we have to get ourselves away from here and fast. I hear sirens." Bryce started the car, u-turned, and headed for the highway.

Clarissa sat staring out the window while tears continued down her cheek. She actually felt nauseous and fought to keep her lunch down. She'd been so close. She almost had them. Damn it. She thought about Jeremy's face. He was so angry and looked at her like he hated her. Ben had obviously been telling him terrible things about her for him to look at her like that. And Sean, he had looked lost and frightened. He'd been crying as they drove off. She just kept replaying the scene over and over in her head not paying any attention to where they were going.

She noticed they were inland by the sunny skies. She continued looking out the window and brushing away the tears pouring from her eyes. They got off the freeway and Clarissa looked to see where they were. There were hills everywhere and they drove down a small road that led them to an even smaller road. The surrounding grass was golden from the sun. There were rolling hills with vineyards stretching across and on top of the hill gigantic windmills stood like decorations. They pulled off the road onto a dirt track that led farther into the hills. Eventually, Bryce stopped in front of a small white cottage and turned the ignition off. He turned to Clarissa.

"Clarissa, I know things didn't go as we had planned. And we're sort of in a tough spot since we've blown our cover. But this isn't the end. I'm not done. And after seeing those boys today, I am even more determined to get them back to you, okay?"

He took her hand in his.

Clarissa looked up and the tears wouldn't come. She couldn't cry anymore. She cleared her throat and said, "I was so close. Seeing them just made it even worse. What will happen now? Won't Ben take them away? I mean, how can we get to them now? He'll surely double their bodyguards. I don't know Bryce, I am feeling so desolate."

"Come on." Bryce left the car and walked to the door. He opened the door and pulled Clarissa into the house. It was nice, although sparsely decorated. The huge couch in the family room is where Clarissa finally succumbed completely to her sorrow. She was having a hard time breathing as she cried. Bryce put a glass in her hand, "Drink."

She downed the brown liquid and felt the burning all the way down her throat. He put more liquor in the glass and handed it to her again. After about four shots she began to feel the warmth easing the sorrow and she lay down on the couch, hiccupped once, and fell asleep.

 ELEVEN

Clarissa awoke to cotton mouth and the sun in her eyes. She slowly registered her surroundings and let the pieces of the previous day fall into place. She felt her heart like a weight in her chest and remembered the events of yesterday. She could hear movement in the kitchen and assumed Bryce must be making breakfast. She swung her feet to the floor and slowly rose from the couch. When she got to the kitchen she could smell coffee and bacon.

"Good morning." Bryce was dressed and obviously had showered as his hair was still damp. "How you doing?"

"Well it feels like I slept with cotton in my mouth and my head is pounding. What did you give me last night?"

"Bourbon. It seemed the best idea at the time. I wasn't thinking too far in the future on that one. Just thought you might want to...."

"Die for a while?" Clarissa chuckled.

"Something like that. You want some breakfast?"

"I'm not sure. Let me take a shower and see how I feel."

"There are extra clothes and things in the closet in the bathroom. I brought us a bag just in case." Bryce turned and looked at Clarissa registering the flinch her body made.

"Okay, thanks." Clarissa made her way down the hall and found the bathroom. In the cupboard was her small duffle bag with her personal items. She was happy to see them. She took a long shower standing under the hot water just letting things seep into her mind. She kept seeing Sean's face and the fear and worry that he showed. It made her think that he might be willing to come to her if she could talk to him. Clarissa hurried through the last part of her shower as her plan came together. She found the prepaid cell phone in her bag and dialed Sean's number. She put a towel on the floor and shoved it up against the crack under the door so Bryce couldn't hear her. Clarissa knew she probably shouldn't be doing this, but she couldn't help herself. The phone rang and Sean's voice surprised Clarissa, she'd been expecting voicemail.

"Sean?"

"Mom, is that you?"

"Yes, sweetie, it's me. Are you okay?" Clarissa could hear muffled noises and she panicked thinking Sean was handing the phone to Ben.

Sean came back on the phone and he was whispering. "Mom? What happened yesterday? Who were those guys and what were you doing?"

"Honey, I'm sorry if you were scared...."

Sean cut her off. "I wasn't scared. I was just confused about what was happening. What was happening?"

"I was trying to get you and Jeremy to come with me. We need to talk." Clarissa thought this was a huge oversimplification.

"Mom, it's kinda creepy here. Jeremy is like a stepford kid with Dad. He does whatever he wants and Dad seems to have gone a little cuckoo too. He's always talking about the future and where we're going. Kinda like Jeremy and I are special or necessary. It's weird. And Dad is always gone. It's really just me and Jeremy and our bodyguards. Which is also weird, why do we have bodyguards?"

"Sean, listen to me. I only have a short time or they will trace this call. Your dad is mixed up in something bad. And he wants to drag you into this too. I was there yesterday to get you and Jeremy out and to bring you home with me. But the bodyguards shot Tony instead."

"Who's Tony?"

"He is a specialist in getting people out of cults and he was there...."

"Wait, you think we're in a cult? Is that what Dad is part of?" Sean paused for a long time.

"Sean. You still there?" Clarissa held the phone away and took a deep breath thinking how to tell her son what was going on. "Your dad is mixed up in something that isn't good. I want you to get away from him because I am worried he is going to take you boys away and I'll never get to see you again. Have you noticed anything else odd going on?" Clarissa saw on her watch she had less than thirty seconds to talk.

"Well, there's a lot of people that come and meet with dad when he's here. Like I said, he's gone a lot too. He doesn't seem to go to work anymore. He's always buying me and Jeremy stuff. And he talks about Idaho a lot. Is that where he wants to take us? To Idaho?" Sean sounded less than happy about that fact.

"I think so. The group your dad belongs to is dangerous, Sean. You cannot let him or Jeremy know you talked to me. Where are you staying?"

"We're at a house up in the hills in Los Gatos. It belongs to some guy Dad knows. He said we're not going to back to school. Instead some guy will come and teach us. You know, Jeremy is totally pals with Dad. And for some reason he believes all the stuff Dad keeps saying about you. I don't though, Mom. I miss you. Can't you come and get me?"

Clarissa's heart was breaking. "Not right now, Sean. But please keep me posted. You'll probably lose this phone after talking to me. But make sure and text me the right number okay...or I'll find it. Honey, I love you. And I'm going to get you out of there! I promise that."

"I love you too, Mom. I gotta go. Someone's coming." The phone went dead.

Clarissa sat on the edge of the bathtub. Her heart was beating fast and she was smiling like crazy having had the opportunity to talk to her son. She felt a surge of strength. She was going to do this. Whatever it took and whatever they had to do, she was going to make this happen. Something in her heart clicked and she just knew that this whole situation, as horrible as it appeared, was going to go her way.

When she opened the door Bryce was standing outside.

"Hi." Clarissa tried to sound nonchalant.

"What are you doing?" Bryce's expression was not happy.

"I took a shower. I feel better and I'm hungry. Is there some food left?

"Clarissa, you called Sean didn't you?"

"What? No...."

"I can see the call. I'm monitoring cell traffic. I tuned in to the call and listened."

"You listened to my call to my son?" Clarissa pushed past him.

"Clarissa. You don't get it, do you? You're not just dealing with your ex-husband but his entire organization, and they are armed and very, very dangerous. You waltzing in and using your feminine wiles is not going to be effective. Do you get it? They shot and killed Tony without any qualms. They would do the same to you. Shoot you...kill you...dead." Bryce pulled her back by the hair.

Clarissa was taken aback as Bryce brought her to him by her hair, spun her around to face him, and then pressed a gun to her temple. The gun was big, black, and very cold. She could feel the chills going through her body at the look in Bryce's eyes. It was stone-cold with absolutely no emotion. Bryce was always aloof, but this was different. He had no feelings and no remorse. He leaned in and whispered in her ear.

"If I pulled the trigger right now the bullet would enter your brain. Your body would immediately go into shock so you might not feel any pain, unless the bullet hit a nerve which means it would be excruciatingly painful. Depending on where the bullet ended up going, you would either die or be paralyzed. Whatever the case, the sound of the shot is so loud near your ear that you would instantly void and maybe even release your bowels. None of this is pleasant and it is more than likely fatal. However, if I chose to shoot you here...." Bryce moved his gun to her hand. "Then it wouldn't kill you but simply maim you with a great amount of pain. Think about being shot in every extremity and the pain you would have to endure. This is the kind of person you are dealing with. Am I making myself clear?" Bryce pulled his gun away and put it into his holster. He stepped back one step and Clarissa pulled away.

Clarissa's eyes were wet. She stood there silent for a moment then looked up at Bryce and asked, "Why did you do that?"

"Because you have to know what you're dealing with. These guys are not pansies who don't want to shoot a woman. They are hardcore, cutthroat killers and your ex is the worst of the bunch. Don't call your son again. Clear?"

Clarissa's words caught in her throat. "Yes."

Bryce turned and walked down the hall and Clarissa slid down the wall to the floor. Her heart was pounding and her palms felt clammy. She couldn't believe that Bryce had just been so calm while holding a gun to her head. What if it had gone off? She was pissed, but then frightened. There was no way to read this man. Clarissa thought they had grown closer but she just realized that his ability to connect to anyone was grossly damaged. While Clarissa wanted to think that he was doing all this not only for the money but because of the cause of saving her children. The fact was he was methodical, calculating, and unreadable. This realization scared Clarissa to death.

Twelve

A couple days went by with Clarissa trying to avoid Bryce. She was pissed at him for his behavior in the hall. She admitted to herself that she didn't know Bryce Brightman at all. Being with him the last few months did not mean she knew him. Obviously you never really knew anyone, look at her ex-husband. Clarissa had spent most of her life with him loving him, and raising their boys. But she had been completely blind to who he was.

Bryce had been in the FBI for over twenty years and Clarissa assumed he had seen things she would not only never understand, but never want to know. It had to affect him. It also explained his robotic way of being. She had noticed it before, but being consumed with finding her sons she really didn't care about how he acted as long as her sons came home. But now that she was pissed she wanted him to react. He didn't though. He was courteous while dismissive, ran her through drills, made her practice shooting, made them meals, and kept to himself.

At night she would listen to see if she could hear him talking on the phone to anyone, but he never did. It was as if he didn't need anyone to live. But he had a son and Clarissa had heard how his voice changed slightly when he mentioned him, so that had to be his tender spot and if Clarissa was going to break his shell then she'd talk about his son.

Bryce came in the door, looked at the kitchen, and frowned. Clarissa was cooking and that meant that every pan, dish, and utensil was now in use. He walked toward her and she turned with a spoon filled with spaghetti sauce, "Taste this."

Bryce flinched and took the spoon she extended. "That's good. Did it take every bowl in the kitchen to make it though?" And he was back to frowning. "Listen, it seems your ex is more thorough than we thought. There was no mention of the situation at the school and that would've been hard to keep contained. That means he has some pull with media. Just more weight to his reach and pull. I only found one small comment about an incident at a local school, but it was gone the next day. So...."

Clarissa dealt with the mess first. "I know I make a mess when I cook. But it's worth it, I promise. Regarding the news, if we don't hear about it that's bad, right?"

"Yes, it's bad."

Clarissa nodded and continued stirring. "Well, so you hungry?"

Bryce sniffed the air. "What smells so good?"

"Cornbread. You had a box of cornmeal in the cupboard so I got creative. You are hungry, right? Do you want a drink? Where've you been?"

"One question at a time, okay?" Bryce opened the fridge and took a soda out which effectively erased one question from Clarissa's list.

"I was thinking we could eat and talk. We haven't really talked about anything other than getting the boys back. I realized that was kind of selfish of me."

"No, it wasn't selfish it was what you hired me for. I'm gonna take a shower before dinner." Bryce headed down the hallway and Clarissa watched him go.

"Woo, he's gonna be a tough nut to crack," she muttered.

Half an hour later the food was almost ready and Bryce was freshly showered and clean. He set the table and then Clarissa found the last remaining bowls to serve dinner in and headed to her seat. They both sat down awkwardly and so Clarissa said, "Bon Appétit."

"It smells good." Bryce heaped pasta and sauce on his plate. He took a piece of warm cornbread, smelling it before he set it on his plate. "What do I smell? It smells like honey and flowers."

Clarissa smiled, "Very good. Its honey lavender butter. I found the honey in the cupboard and picked some lavender outside and steeped the honey in it. Do you like it?" She waited to see what his reaction would be.

Bryce took a bite of the cornbread which he had dabbed with the flavored butter. His face was a bit squinched up but as he took a bite he paused, and Clarissa could tell he liked it. She smiled and started eating.

"So, Bryce. I know we haven't been exactly talking a lot lately. I have to say I was mad at you after you pulled a gun on me."

Bryce looked at her without blinking.

"I decided that what you said had merit, even if the way you said it was a bit brutish. But tonight I thought we could just talk like normal people, is that a possiblity?"

"Is it possible for us to be normal?" A smile played at his lips.

"Well, maybe normal might be hard, but we could at least get to know each other. What do you think?"

"Clarissa, I get that you are a woman so that means that you like to talk about stuff and share. But I don't work that way. First off, you are a job. I am working for you, so getting touchy feely is not gonna happen. Second, I'm not a guy that shares his feelings. It's not personal. I just have learned not to be obvious about my thoughts and emotions, much to my ex-wife's chagrin. So talking about things is not a way to get to know me since I am not going to share myself."

"Is that why you got divorced?"

"Partly. There was also the fact that we didn't have much in common. And I wasn't home a lot and she wanted me to react to stuff. You know, at Christmas she wanted me to be thrilled about the gift she got me. I was. I liked it. I just didn't show it the way she wanted. I think she needed more from me; more that I didn't have to give or didn't understand how to do. The job was my life and I probably shouldn't have gotten married in the first place. A lot of guys lose their marriages. But I guess I thought I was different. Turns out I wasn't. But the best thing about being married was having my son. He's great."

"Tell me about him. How old is he?" Clarissa saw a small crack in the exterior but she wasn't sure she could pry her fingers through to get to him.

"He's thirteen. Smart. He looks like his mom. He's got a good head on his shoulders. He understands my life and doesn't hold it against me. That's a big thing for a kid. I see him as much as I can and we enjoy hanging out."

Clarissa was silent and tears began to

form.

"I know you miss your boys." Bryce reached for her hand and squeezed it.

"Thank you, Bryce. I do. And talking to Sean the other day, well, it just made it worse. He's scared. He needs me and I'm not doing anything to help."

"You are. I've been working on the next plan. Tim is in. And I spoke to someone else you know."

"Who?"

"Dan. He said he'd help us. He knows the circumstances and he's strong in abduction techniques so he is actually the perfect guy for the team."

"But how are we going to get the boys out when they know who we are and that we're coming? We lost the element of surprise."

Bryce smiled, "That's what I was hoping you'd say. I have an idea." Bryce continued talking for about forty-five minutes explaining the plan to Clarissa and she had to say it sounded pretty good. She started picking up the plates and Bryce joined her in the kitchen. "You don't have to help me. I made a huge mess. I'll clean it up."

"No, I'll do it. You go and take a bath or something and I'll be done when you get back. I have a surprise for you."

"A surprise?" These words made her heart leap. It had been ages since she'd felt anything move her and she couldn't help but be excited.

Clarissa lay in the tub soaking and thinking. She had gotten a little bit of information out of Bryce, but the vault was well guarded and she was relatively sure that she couldn't break in. It was weird too. She should be attracted to this man. He was good looking and had the whole knight-in-shining-armor-coming-to-her-rescue thing going for him, but there was something that kept any kind of romance off the table. Clarissa padded down the hallway in sweats and a shirt and turned the corner to bowls, spoons, toppings and ice cream sitting on the table.

"Oh my gosh, where did this come from?" Clarissa was giddy with joy.

"Well, I figured it was the least I could do after holding a gun to your head."

"I accept your apology." Clarissa dug into one of the quarts of ice cream taking a bite and rolling her eyes in ecstasy. "You gonna join me?"

"Of course. I may be tough, but I am human. Ice cream is the absolute perfect food on earth. There's cookie dough pieces in the bowl there."

"Seriously? Give 'em."

They both sat down on the couch and dug into the treat. Their contented sighs mingled.

"But wait...there's more." He pulled out a remote and turned the television on. The music started and Clarissa screamed.

"Animal House? I freaking love this movie."

Bryce looked pleased and they both lost themselves in the antics of the movie and the tastes of the ice cream. When the movie ended Clarissa was asleep. Bryce turned off the TV and lifted Clarissa off the couch. He walked to her bedroom and lay her down on the bed then covered her with a quilt. He paused and watched her as she moved settling into the bed. For a moment an unguarded look of caring crossed his face. He caught himself, moved out the door, and down the hallway.

Clarissa woke up and stretched. She remembered the night before and was suddenly aware she was in her bed. "He must've carried me here," she said under her breath. A smile broke across her face.

The sun was shining and she could hear him talking to someone. Clarissa dressed quickly in jeans and a denim shirt and made her way to the kitchen.

"Hi, Clarissa." Dan stood up and hugged her. "Bryce fill you in?"

"He told me you were going to help us get my sons. Said you had experience with abduction cases."

"Yep, I do. Did a lot of those kinds of cases on the job. Anyway, from the intelligence I have from Bryce I think that our best bet is to grab them when they're out, obviously. We'll work all the logistics out so that it goes seamlessly. I know last time there was issues, but we aren't going to have that problem again, okay?"

His surety made Clarissa feel better. "Okay. I need some coffee."

Later that day Clarissa decided she needed to get out of this homestead. She wanted to get some things at the store and she needed items that she didn't feel comfortable asking Bryce to get for her. She found him working in the barn. "Bryce, I need to go to the store, okay?"

"Can't I go for you?"

"No, I need to get some things I don't think you want to buy for me." Clarissa raised her eyebrows at him.

"Oh. How about I drive you in and wait outside. That be enough privacy? I don't want you driving into town alone." Bryce wasn't going to budge on that point.

"Well, if that's my option, let's go."

"Give me ten minutes and I'll be ready."

Clarissa got her purse and some cash she had taken from the safety deposit box. She was sitting on the couch waiting when Bryce walked in. "Ready to go, eh?" He smiled.

Twenty minutes later Clarissa was looking at the downtown area of a small but bustling place called Livermore. The main street was quaint and filled with little boutiques, restaurants, and coffee houses. Clarissa looked at the stores and told Bryce she didn't think she could find the things she needed here. He redirected the truck and soon they were pulling in the Target parking lot. Clarissa got out of the car and

THE X   *173*

Bryce began to get out too.

"Bryce, please. I won't be long, okay. And I'll be very careful. I have this." She pointed to the pendant around her neck. "I have my phone out in my hand ready to push the instant dial." She showed her thumb on the button.

"Okay, go ahead. I'll wait here. How long do you think you'll be?"

"About twenty minutes tops. I promise." The door shut and Clarissa felt herself bouncing toward the entrance. Once inside the doors she stopped and asked if there were pay phones she could use. The boy behind the counter looked confused. He took a phone from behind his counter and held it out to her. Clarissa felt this would be safe. She dialed Becky's number and waited. She got a message and sadly hung up without saying anything. Then she got her cart and headed into the blissful twenty minutes of shopping...alone.

Bryce sat in the car listening to the radio and frequently looking from his phone to the front door. After about twenty-five minutes he called Clarissa's phone. It rang four times and a voice said, "Hello."

"Clarissa?" He thought she sounded funny. "You okay?"

"This isn't Clarissa. I saw a phone lying on the ground and when it started ringing I picked it up. I'm Michele. Who's this?"

Bryce sat up and said, "Is there a woman near there in her late forties, brownish hair?"

"No, hang on....no. I just looked around the other aisle. Hello...hello." The lady yelled into the phone. "Hello...are you there?"

Bryce sprinted into the store. He ran down each aisle mentally beating himself up for letting Clarissa go in alone. He should have just followed her from a distance. "Damn," he uttered under his breath. Once he checked all the aisles he went through the doors to the backroom. No one appeared to be back there and he traversed the whole area before he ran into someone with a red shirt.

"Sir, you aren't supposed to be back here. Are you lost?"

"No, listen you need to call security. There has been a kidnapping."

The girl stared at him.

Bryce yelled in her face. "Get on your walkie talkie and get me the head of your security right now. A woman has been abducted from your store and we have to act fast."

Baffled the girl spoke into the walkie talkie, "Bert? We gotta problem in the back room. Can you meet me at exit six please? Sir, can you follow me."

They walked a bit before emerging from one of the doors to four guys dressed in red shirts with walkie talkies strapped to their belts. "Sir, you said something about kidnapping?"

"Yes, I am ex-FBI and I had a client that came into the store to buy a couple things. That was a half an hour ago. Her phone was found on an aisle at the front of the store which makes me think she was snatched, probably brought out through a back exit since I was sitting in the front. Can you show me where someone could exit around here?"

"Sir, you're going to have to come with me to the office and fill out a complaint and we'll have to call the police. Can you follow me?" The biggest and oldest guy reached for Bryce's arm.

"Listen, I am sure you think I might be a crazy loon but call Detective Ridder at the Livermore Police department and he'll square who I am. But I don't have time to go to the office and fill out paperwork. I gotta see what's going on."

With that Bryce took off running looking for an exit in the back. He found a door that led to a loading dock and on the ground was a matchbook. That was a clue that Bryce had taught Clarissa to do. "Damn it." He looked back and forth and heard sirens coming from a distance.

The big security guys found him and grabbed both his arms. He decided rather than lay them all out flat he'd just go with them so he had a chance to see the security footage of the loading dock. He was sitting in a red chair when Detective Ridder walked in.

"Bryce. Good to see you." The detective nodded at the security officer. "So, what's going on here?"

The security officer started to tell the facts and Detective Ridder listened and nodded then he said, "Thank you, Jeffery. It's Jeffery, right? I'm going to talk to this gentleman alone, okay?"

Jeffery seemed relieved to pass this powder keg off to the cops. Detective Ridder slapped him on the back as he left the room. He turned to Bryce. "What's up?"

"Listen we need to get a look at all the security cameras in the back area and the loading dock. Someone abducted my client."

"You're sure?"

Bryce nodded. "Her phone was found in an aisle. They didn't come out the front because I was watching the front. And my client left a clue with a matchbook so I know she went out that way."

"Hang tight, I'm gonna get us access." He left the room and Bryce sat there chastising himself. He knew better. He should've just gone with her. A moment later Detective Ridder stuck his head in and said, "Follow me."

They walked down the hall and entered a darkened room. Bryce's eyes had to adjust. When they did he noticed there was a whole wall filled with monitors and the picture changed every five to ten seconds. Bryce panned the monitors to find the one he was looking for. When he saw the loading dock he asked for that one to be run back. Ten minutes later he had met Clarissa's ex, at least by sight. The black SUV that had been at the school lot had pulled up to the loading dock and a man had gotten out. He was not tall, but held himself with the confidence of one that knew something everyone else didn't. A moment later a big guy exited the stores back door and was holding Clarissa's limp body. Obviously she had done what he'd shown her and fainted. As he zoomed in on the screen he saw her reach into her pocket and drop the matchbook. The two men were joined by a third and they opened the back and put Clarissa inside. As the door closed Bryce saw Clarissa look up at the camera, and she looked scared.

Thirteen

Clarissa began to wake up. She could feel something over her head. It was hard to breathe. Her hands were tied, but she used the technique Bryce had shown her to work at the tethers until she could slide one hand out. She pulled the mask off her face and took deep breaths. Looking around she tried to get her bearings. She was in a small room, sitting on a shipping crate with a blanket on it.

Bryce's voice was in her head and she began muttering his training. "Get your bearings. What do you know?"

She slowly raised herself to a sitting

position. Her head was aching which meant she had probably been given chloroform. Clarissa rubbed her wrists where she had been tied. She tucked the leather strap into her pocket as she might be able to use it later. She stood slowly getting her equilibrium. "Damn, Bryce is gonna be so pissed."

The room was dingy and smelled like mold. The window had been painted with grey paint on the outside so she couldn't see out and dimmed the light in the room. She looked around for anything that could give her clues to where she was. She listened next to the window to hear the sound of traffic, but it was silent. Making her way to the only door she got down on the floor to see what was on the other side. All she could see was sunlight and a room that had a blue painted floor. Standing up made her head hurt so bad she had to sit down.

Clarissa didn't know how long she had been asleep, but it seemed late afternoon given the light she could see under the door. Rubbing her eyes she could hear her stomach growling. As if on cue she heard a rattling at the door handle. She grabbed the tether from her pocket and wound it round her hands as she lay down on the crate. The door opened and she saw a form in the doorway. Clarissa recognized one of the goons that had been with Sean and Jeremy. He pushed a tray across the floor until it hit the crate. The noise startled Clarissa and she jumped. "Hey, I have to go to the bathroom."

He paused at the door. "What?"

"I have to go to the bathroom."

"Wait a minute." He shut the door and she heard the sound of the lock. Clarissa jumped off the crate and knelt by the door looking underneath it.

"Yeah, what are we supposed to do if she has to go to the bathroom? You want me to take her down?" He nodded, grunted an assent, and closed the phone.

Clarissa ran back to the crate being careful not to step on the food. It looked like a fast food burger and a drink. She began salivating even at the meager fare. The door clicked open and the massive man was back.

"Finish your food and when you're done I'll take you to the john."

Clarissa nodded and the door shut. A few minutes later she heard his footsteps returning and she stood up.

The door opened but it wasn't the man she had seen before, it was her ex-husband,

Ben.

"Hi, Clarissa. You've been a pain in the ass, haven't you?"

"Ben, why did you kidnap me?" Clarissa stared at him, "Who the hell are you?"

"Well, right now I'm your worst nightmare. You know, you've never known when to let a subject go. You always wanted to discuss things to the 'nth degree. But this time I don't need to consider what you want. You're here because you got in the way and I need you to stay put and shut up until I can accomplish what it is I need to do. If you stay quiet then I will let you go, but if you cause any more problems then I will..." He paused and stepped closer pulling a gun from his jacket pocket.

Clarissa slid farther across the crate. "What? Are you gonna shoot me? You're going to kill the mother of your sons? Really? 'Cause if that's all you wanted why didn't you do it when you were in our house?" Clarissa stood up and moved forward.

"Clarissa, I didn't kill you because I didn't think you would be a problem. But now you've become one. I don't intend on letting you fuck up everything I've been working for." Ben screwed the silencer onto the barrel.

Quickly Clarissa surmised that she must be somewhere near people because he was worried about the sound the gun would make. Ben moved towards her pointing the gun at her face. She silently thanked Bryce for his recent introduction to firearms so close to her head because she felt strangely calm while she was working out what to do next. Ben drew closer and pointed the gun at her forehead. Clarissa was thinking about which defensive maneuver to use against him when she felt something around her neck. The necklace Bryce had given her rubbed against Ben's arm and reminded her that Bryce could find her. Her mind whirred and she determined that she might be able to get information that would allow her and the group to find the boys before Ben took off with them. So she calmed herself enough to go a bit slack and decided fear might be a good tactic.

"Ben, I just want the boys. You can do whatever you need to do and I will never bother you again, but please, I need my boys." Clarissa tried to sound pathetic knowing that Ben reacted to that tone.

"I need the boys more than you do. They are part of the plan so you getting them back is not an option. The quicker you realize this and let go, the better it will be for all of us. Do you know how hard Sean cried the other night and the confusion was so hurtful to him. Do you realize what you're doing to him?" Ben had let go of her neck and stepped back, but he was still pointing the gun at her.

"But what do they believe about me? What have you told them?" Clarissa realized she could get more from Ben if he thought she really didn't know what he was doing so she decided submission would serve her well. "I just want them to love me and know I love them."

"They do, well sort of." Ben shrugged his shoulders.

"What have you told them, Ben?"

"Look it doesn't matter, in a couple of days all this will be moot."

Clarissa chose her next words carefully. If she said too much then he would shut down. "Is Sean okay?"

Ben lowered the gun from Clarissa's head feeling that he had achieved the upper hand and had effectively frightened her.

"Yes, he's fine. I'm not going to hurt them, Clarissa. I am actually going to give them more than they ever could hope to attain by themselves. I am doing all this for the boys."

"Could I see them? Just once, please? Ben, I will leave you alone and them too if I could just see them both again. Would that be possible? Please, I'm begging you."

Ben considered the statement while walking to the door. "If you keep quiet here and don't make a fuss then perhaps that could be arranged. But it all depends on you." He knocked and the door opened. He left and Clarissa heard him lock it behind him.

Clarissa felt a stir of joy, "Yes, I understand. I won't be any more trouble. I promise. If I get to see the boys, then I will be the model prisoner."

"Well, let's see how it goes the next day or so. If I believe you are sincere then I will bring the boys to you before we leave for the airport."

Clarissa's eyes narrowed for just a moment. Now she knew that Ben and the boys were leaving soon. This fact would help in timing when she and the guys moved against Ben. Clarissa felt her heart beat a little faster thinking that they had a chance now of getting her boys back. The only problem was Bryce would be coming to get her, so how did she convey to him that she would have the perfect chance to steal the boys back if she sat tight? She looked around the room. The windows were facing out and not a lot of light was coming through them. If she could write something on them then maybe she could let Bryce know not to storm in and rescue her.

Reaching in her pocket she pulled out her lipstick. It was red which meant it could show up if she wrote on the glass; the problem was that anyone in the room could see the message too. She looked for something to write on. There was some cardboard she could use, but could she get it out the window? There was only a small space where the window was open so air was allowed to come through. How could she be sure that Bryce would see it before making a charge into the building? Clarissa thought about how Bryce did everything. He was always methodical about knowing all the entrances and exits, so he would probably scope out the building before he did anything. She'd have to go on faith that the note she wrote would be found by him or one of the guys. She wrote on the cardboard, *Boys coming here in couple of days. Don't get me, get them.*

She pushed the cardboard through the small slit and it almost fell when she lost her grip on it. Luckily, she pulled it back through the window. That meant she needed to tie something to the cardboard in case she dropped it. She had one chance and she couldn't screw it up. She looked for something to use and found some packing straw. She pulled a few pieces and braided them making them stronger. She worked to poke a hole through the cardboard with her nail. Because she hadn't been able to get her nails done they were really long. She threaded the braided straw through the hole, then she lowered the cardboard to the ground propping it against the wall. Gently, she pulled the straw back and the cardboard thankfully stayed propped up with the red lipstick facing out. Now she'd have to wait... and pray.

Bryce had the intel he needed to confirm who had taken Clarissa. He headed to the car and opened the glove compartment. Extracting a black square he flipped a switch and heard the wonderful beeping sound. He pulled out his phone and attached the instrument to it. A map appeared on his screen and he could see the blinking light of Clarissa's beacon. "Got ya."

Bryce dialed his cell phone and paused until he heard a click. "I found her. Listen we gotta get the crew together. I think besides getting her out we need to get Ben and use him as leverage to get the boys back. But I have the address so let's get over there and scan the building. I'll text you the address."

Back at the house he retrieved his supplies. He hadn't thrown everything into the truck since he'd expected just to be on a short shopping trip. He changed his clothes and threw a sweatshirt and sweatpants in for Clarissa. He retrieved his black bag from the barn and contacted his guys again. They were going to meet him at the address and formulate a plan once they'd done surveillance on the building.

An hour later they had mapped out the entire perimeter. Dan had gotten a set of blueprints from a friend of his so they knew the layout of the inside as well. The corporation that owned the property was part of Ben's group. Bryce had a nagging feeling though. As much as they were talking about storming the front and getting Clarissa out, he kept putting it off by telling them to check the outside one more time

The guys were wondering why he was stalling, but they did what he said. That was how ten minutes into the next scan they found the note Clarissa had left.

Bryce smiled. "Dang." He was impressed at her thinking. Now he knew where she was he had a sense of timing for the action.

"Now that we have the note we know that we have the chance to snag the boys. But that means patience as we wait to see when Ben's gonna arrive. You guys cool with that?"

Both Dan and Tim nodded as they settled down against the wall. Dan took out a thermos and filled his cup. He motioned towards Tim, but Tim shook his head and pulled his hood over his head. "You want one, Bryce?"

"Sure. What is it?"

"Coffee, black and strong."

"Thanks." Bryce took a cup and took a whiff confirming the strength of the brew.

"So, you got it all worked out now? You know where she's at?" Dan nodded to the outside towards the building.

"Well, waiting for dark is best, but I saw a black SUV parked at the North entrance so they aren't being careful about where they park. I don't think Ben expects us to find her so he's just taking basic precautions. But I'm not gonna assume. Once it gets darker I'll use the infrared to get a pulse on how many guys are in there with her. Tim is checking on security systems to see if one is running to the building. My guess is there isn't, but better safe than sorry."

"So, what's the deal here? You like this girl?" Dan winked at him.

"No. I mean, she's a pretty tough cookie and you know I have a weakness for that. But I guess I keep figuring that if it was my boy I would feel just like her. I want to get her sons back to her. She's naive and I feel a little sorry for her."

"That's it? You don't want to...or have you done that already?" Dan winked again.

"Dan, she's attractive, but she's a client and that's all." Bryce turned away to end the conversation but he was thinking if maybe Dan wasn't right. He was attracted to Clarissa, but he hadn't done anything because he never mixed business with pleasure. But this time he'd had to struggle not to kiss her. He knew that any relationship built this way never panned out because there's a weird dynamic when a distraught, worried woman gets emotionally tied to the man coming in to save her kids. He'd seen enough of those affairs happen and fizzle in the field and he wasn't one not to pay attention to lessons learned. As the room got darker he pulled out the infrared and started to scan the building.

Clarissa kept her eyes glued out the window looking for some sign that Bryce was around. She thought she saw movement earlier in the night but it turned out to be a raccoon's eyes that caught the moonlight. Yet as she crouched by the window she just felt he must be near. She said another silent prayer to add to the thousand she'd already uttered. "Please let him see my note."

Bryce had picked up only one guy in a room outside of where Clarissa was. One guard. *Damn, Ben was confident, wasn't he?* As the light began to edge through the sky

Tim and Dan roused and they sat down to business. They spent two hours working out every logistic with not only the perimeter but using the plans to know how to move once inside the building. Timing was the biggest factor. Because they didn't know when Ben was coming they were going to have to take up positions soon and simply wait for him to show up. The guys geared up with headphones and all the equipment they would need. Dan had thought ahead and pulled two more thermoses out of his bag and a sack of MRI's. They suited up and headed out still under the cover of darkness.

Clarissa had dozed but awoke with a start. Someone was out there. She quickly stuck her eyes to the window slit and sure enough saw a man moving towards the building in the umbrage of early morning. Clarissa was thrilled. It was Bryce coming to get the boys, but immediately the joy turned to terror as she assumed he was coming to get her. He hadn't seen her note. She felt the tears welling up in her eyes from the stress of worry, no food, and defeat as she knew she'd be saved but her boys wouldn't. She heard a scuttling at the window and wondered if the raccoon had returned.

"Clarissa." A whisper moved towards her.

She looked out. "Bryce?"

"Yep, it's me."

"You didn't see my note? Ben is going to bring the boys here on their way to the airport. It's the perfect chance to get them both."

"Yeah, I know. I've got the guys set up so that we can move as soon as he shows up. Don't worry. We've got it all worked out. You just keep calm. Are you okay?"

Clarissa nodded and said, "Yes, I'm tired and hungry. But I'm good."

Bryce stuck two protein bars through the window slit. "Here, these will help."

"Got any coffee?"

Bryce smiled, "Yes, but I don't think I can fit the thermos through the window."

"Okay, I'm happy with the protein bars."

"So now you know we've got you covered. Just hang tight."

Clarissa was quiet for a moment as she chewed a protein bar. "Bryce?" There was no response. "Bryce?" Clarissa whispered again.

"Yes."

"Thanks."

"You're welcome. Now stay quiet and try to get some rest. You'll need your strength."

Clarissa heard him move away from the window and she felt her eyes shutting. Knowing Bryce was here she could finally relax a bit and fell asleep in seconds.

FOURTEEN

The rattle of the doorknob woke Clarissa immediately. She jumped up and moved to the crate sitting demurely when the door opened. The bodyguard was in the doorway holding a tray. "You gonna eat today?"

Clarissa nodded and said, "Can I use the restroom?"

He nodded and motioned for her to exit the room. Clarissa walked fast. Once in the bathroom she looked for a weapon and found a pencil in the medicine cabinet. She put it in her bra and exited following the bodyguard to her room. As the bodyguard went to leave she said, "Excuse me, do you know when Ben is coming? Is it today?"

The bodyguard ignored her, shut the door, and locked it.

The day dragged on. Clarissa slept and walked the room over and over. She did push-ups, sit-ups, and triceps lifts off the end of the crate. She meditated and talked to herself. But she felt confident knowing the guys were sitting out there at the ready. She lay on the crate covered in packing straw and slept through the night.

The next morning in the early dawn she heard a sound outside her door. It sounded like footsteps and she raised herself up to listen better. She not only heard footsteps but also heard her son, Sean, asking where she was. Clarissa was up and to the door in a second. In that same moment the door swung open and connected with her head. She fell backwards with a stinging pain in her forehead. She put her hand to her head and felt the sticky warmth of blood.

"Mom, are you okay? Dad, the door hit mom. She's hurt."

Ben stepped in behind Sean and smiled a malicious smile. "Oh, I'm sure she'll live, Sean."

Clarissa ignored the cut and grabbed

Sean to her. "Sean, are you okay. Oh my gosh, I'm so glad to see you." She squeezed him so tight he was struggling to breathe.

"Mom, I can't...breathe." Sean pulled away. "Gosh, you're strong now."

Jeremy walked in behind his dad. He didn't move towards Clarissa immediately, but she saw a flicker of concern when he saw the blood on her forehead. He ducked back out of the door and re-emerged with a wad of wet paper towels and a Band-Aid. "Here, Mom." He handed everything to Clarissa.

"Thank you, Jeremy." Clarissa didn't take a step forward so she didn't make him move away.

Sean was hugging her and whispering in her ear, "We're leaving today, Mom. And I don't think we're coming back. Dad said he'll have his bodyguards let you go once our plane has taken off. Don't worry, he promised you wouldn't be hurt." He stepped back and shook his head to warn her not to say anything.

"Clarissa, I'm going to give you ten minutes with the boys and then I will be back to get them." He shut the door behind him and Clarissa heard the lock click.

Jeremy went to the door and tried

to open it. He stepped back defeated and turned towards Clarissa. "Why did he lock the door?"

"Probably because he doesn't trust me." Clarissa was holding Sean and rubbing his hair. "Jeremy, are you okay?"

Jeremy shrugged, "Of course, why wouldn't I be?" His defensive tone told her that he still bought Ben's bullshit.

"No reason, just checking. Can you come here, please?"

"Why?" He was trying not to make contact with Clarissa that much was apparent.

"Because I only get ten more minutes with you both before you're going wherever your dad is taking you and I love you and don't know how I'm going to live without you both. Is that enough of a reason for you?"

Jeremy seemed shamed and he lowered his head and moved to Clarissa. She grabbed him and hugged him tight. She felt his body slack as he fought to stay removed from her. Eventually he couldn't fight that this was his mother and he began to cry quietly as he clutched Clarissa. She cooed to him, "It's all right."

Clarissa was completely here with her boys but also wondered when Bryce would be making his move. She felt her breath catch as she pushed the boys at arm's length and said, "Listen. You two need to know something. I don't know why your dad is taking you away but I want you both to know that I am not giving up. I love you both more than life and I can't lose you. But for now, I have to be practical and let you go. Know that if you ever want to come home to me the door will be open."

Sean nodded and Jeremy tried not to let his emotions show, but Clarissa could see him nod a little.

As they stood there Clarissa heard a huge boom and heard the glass in the window shake. She moved the boys away from the wall and pulled them down behind the crate. The second boom blew apart the wall where the window had been and pieces of concrete flew everywhere. Jeremy tried to stand up and Clarissa pulled him down shouting, "Jeremy, stay put."

The door to the room flew open and both the bodyguards and Ben ran into the room. Clarissa had her hand on Jeremy's arm as Bryce and Dan jumped through the hole in the wall. Dan grabbed Jeremy and threw a hood over him then grabbed his hand and legs and threw him over his back in a fireman's carry. Jeremy tried to wiggle free, but Dan was too strong for the teenage boy. Ben saw Dan leaving through the wall and snatched Sean's arm away from Clarissa. He pulled Sean out with him.

"Bryce, he has Sean. Get Sean." Clarissa ran towards the bodyguard throwing herself headfirst at his legs bringing him down to the ground. She straddled his body and hit his ear with her fist as he shrieked in pain. Then she took the pencil out of her bra and stabbed him in the eye. The bodyguard was screeching with pain on the floor all the while Clarissa was yelling at Bryce, "Get Sean."

Instead Bryce grabbed Clarissa and pulled her out the hole in the wall. One second after they cleared the wall stones fell from above covering the hole they had just exited from. "Bryce, you have to get Sean."

"I will. Follow me." He handed her a gun and she ran behind him.

She saw out of the corner of her eye that Dan had put marine ties around Jeremy's hands and feet and pushed him into the back seat of his van. Then he locked the door with a click and ran towards Bryce and Clarissa. Clarissa was behind the men as they headed to the front of the building. Bryce stopped and put his hand to her chest telling her to stay put. He and Dan ran around the corner and Clarissa's heart was beating erratically. A moment later she heard shots being fired and tried desperately not to think of Sean being shot and lying on the ground.

Finally, Clarissa couldn't wait anymore and came barreling around the corner with her gun drawn. She saw both Dan and Bryce aiming at the SUV and Sean being pushed inside. Then Clarissa stopped cold as she saw Ben aim his gun at her. She hit the ground and a second later she heard a bullet whizz above her head. Bryce saw this and took off running full bore at the SUV. A rope appeared and Tim slid down a line hitting the ground running. Both Bryce and Tim were gaining on the SUV as it began slowly rolling towards the gate. The window on the passenger side opened and Ben began shooting at the two men. Clarissa screamed, "Sean."

They all ran after the SUV as it picked up speed and flew down the street. Bryce yelled, "Get to the van. They gotta be going to the airport. Ben has to want to get out of here with at least one boy."

Once they were in the van Clarissa saw that Jeremy wasn't moving. "Dan, what happened? Did you shoot him? Dan?"

Dan yelled as he flew down the street. "I gave him a shot to knock him out. He's just sleeping. We couldn't have him trying to escape to his dad, could we? He'll be fine."

Clarissa pulled the hood off of his head and saw his face was slack in sleep. She smoothed his hair. "Jeremy, you'll forgive me, won't you?"

Bryce moved from the front seat and took her hand. "Clarissa, he'll be fine. Now let's focus on getting your other son, okay?"

"What do we do?"

"There they are." Dan shouted back.

Bryce and Clarissa moved forward to look out the front window. They could see the black SUV careening down the roads taking corners too quickly. Clarissa was scared they would tip over and crash, but they managed to make it to the airport. Dan was a good driver and stayed far enough back to follow them but not close enough that they would know they were being followed. Tim was strapping a shotgun over his shoulder swaying perfectly with the movement of the car.

Bryce checked his gun, chambering a round. "My guess is they have a private plane so they won't be heading to the main terminal." As the words lingered in the air the SUV turned into the driveway for the private and single engine planes. The SUV had slowed down assuming they hadn't been followed.

Dan pulled up to an office and Bryce jumped out and got into an airport maintenance truck. Clarissa moved up to the van's passenger seat and they continued to follow the SUV as it turned into a hanger. Bryce drove past them and stopped the truck next to the hangar. Dan slowed to a stop behind a gas truck before reaching the hangar. He nodded to Clarissa and she, Dan, and Tim jumped out of the van. Dan locked it and put the keys in his pocket as they moved to the side entrance. Bryce drove the truck into the hangar as Dan pushed the side door open and he, Tim, and Clarissa slunk into the building.

Sitting in the middle of the hangar

was a private jet. The black SUV was about twenty feet away and the driver's and passenger's doors were wide open. Sean was sitting in the back seat and Clarissa moved to go retrieve him when she felt Dan's hand on her arm. "Not yet. Wait."

Bryce in the maintenance truck pulled up to the SUV and got out. He headed towards the office. Ben stood talking at the stairs of the plane to a man who must be the pilot. As Bryce walked towards the office the pilot acknowledged him with a nod, pointed towards the office door, and Ben and the bodyguard turned and looked back at him.

Ben nodded at the bodyguard who strode to the SUV and pulled Sean out by the elbow. Sean looked scared and yet he moved compliantly with the bodyguard towards the plane and his father. The pilot paused and began talking to Ben again while the bodyguard moved toward them. Clarissa and Dan heard a shot and Dan said, "Move now."

They all ran full out. Clarissa had one goal, to get Sean. He was standing there with a surprised look on his face as the bodyguard lay dead at his feet. As Clarissa ran toward him she saw Ben recognize her and move to get Sean. She wasn't going to make it before him since he was closer to their son, but she never slowed her pace. She ran at full speed and could hear Dan and Tim right next to her.

She hit Ben ramming her head straight into his chest. He went sailing backward and she landed on top of him. He had the wind knocked out of him and struggled to push her off. She rolled to the side feeling the impact of her hit in her neck, but tried to shake off the pain while turning to see if Dan or Tim had reached Sean.

Ben moved slowly as he retrieved a gun from his pocket and pointed it at Clarissa. She shook her head putting her hand on her knee to stand up. Ben was still holding the gun on her and looking for Sean.

"Ben, it's over. You are not going to get Sean. I will not allow that."

The gun went off and Clarissa felt something cold then immediately hot in her upper arm. In that instant instead of falling to the floor in pain, she felt the white hot rage of a mother surge through her body. Anger, frustration, worry, and fear combined to create a hulk-like power to rage. She ran straight for Ben as he finally got to his feet, turned, and ran while firing another shot over his shoulder. The shot veered to the left of her head as she continued her pursuit.

Ben turned to face her and line up another shot and she stopped.

He smiled malevolently, "You may have gotten the boys, but you won't get me. I will get them back. You'll have to always look around wondering when they will disappear again."

Clarissa felt the anger subside and calm descend upon her. She took steps toward Ben as he pulled the trigger again, but she didn't stop moving until she reached him. She grabbed him by the wrist, turned her body against him and flipped him over her shoulder. As he lay on the ground she stamped her foot on his hand holding the gun until he let go. She kicked the gun away and then pulled him to his feet. She punched him in the face as hard as she could, being careful to keep her thumb outside her fingers.

The impact made Ben's head bend backward and the surprise in his eyes fueled her attack. She punched him again as blood spurted from his nose and she heard the crack of the bone. He put his hands up to shield his face and she sent an uppercut punch to his side. He buckled over to the left as she punched him again and again. He went down on one knee and she stepped back, cocked her foot, and kicked him square in the face. He paused, swayed, and fell unconscious to the ground.

Clarissa went down on one knee as Dan, Bryce, Tim, and Sean reached her at the same time.

"Mom! Damn, you just kicked dad's ass!" The impression showed strong in his eyes.

Bryce and Dan smiled broadly, helping their student to her feet. As Clarissa swayed, Bryce swung her up into his arms and Dan bent down fastening marine ties to Ben's feet and hands.

The sound of sirens approached and Clarissa could feel the blood returning to her body. She felt weak, but yet strong at the same time. Being held in Bryce's arms was comforting. "Sean, come here."

Sean moved to his mother and grabbed her hands.

"I love you." Clarissa said quietly.

"I love you too, Mom." Sean had tears

in his eyes.

The hangar was soon filled with police, FBI, and other official-looking personnel. Sean was speaking to an FBI agent while Bryce and Dan hovered over Clarissa as the paramedics worked on her arm. Ben's shot had gone straight through so they bandaged her until she would agree to go to the hospital. Tim had snuck out as soon as the police arrived.

They were still answering questions when Dan's van drove up and Tim brought Jeremy out of the back. Jeremy was shaking his head and wobbling as he walked trying to shake off the drug Dan had given him. Tim brought Jeremy over to Clarissa and she hugged her son tight.

After getting cleaned up, Clarissa was brought into a room where Jeremy was sitting behind a desk. Sean was sitting in a chair in the corner. Agents asked Jeremy what he knew about his father's group. It turned out that Jeremy knew more than Sean ever had.

Ben had spent a great deal of time brain-washing Jeremy to believe the mantra of the group and Ben had filled his head with the splendor and riches to be attained when they fulfilled their mission. The FBI had been right, The Truth sect wanted to take over the American presidency. They would do this with financial support from their high-level members who had billions at their disposal. They utilized their political contacts to pick a member that could go the farthest and used local and state government to facilitate finding the right candidate. Turns out Jeremy was going to be the one that they used to achieve this goal. With all the attention from his dad, Jeremy had found himself falling in line with the doctrine. It wasn't until Clarissa had made the attempt to get them back at school and Sean's constant persuasion that Jeremy began to have doubts.

Hours later their interrogations were done, their father had been taken into custody, and they were free to go home. Clarissa stood stunned not sure where home was anymore. Bryce told her to go to the cabin and stay for a bit getting back to normal and spending time with her sons. She hugged him thankfully and Dan offered his van as the small family piled inside and headed to the outskirts of suburbia to detox and reacquaint.

FIFTEEN

A few nights later, Bryce found himself driving up the dirt road to a house filled with light. He knocked on the door and Jeremy opened it. He smiled at the sight of Bryce and pulled him inside. "Thanks, man. My mom told me everything you did for her and for us. Thanks." Jeremy put his hand out and Bryce took it and shook it.

"No problem. I'm glad you're safe. Everything going okay?"

"I have some headaches once in a while, but I'm feeling pretty good. And after spending time with my Mom I get what was going on. I think maybe my Dad was giving me something, a drug or something, 'cause I always felt a little edgy and had a really short temper. That's gone now, so I feel more like myself. My mom's in the kitchen."

Jeremy headed to the back yelling out for Sean.

As Bryce turned the corner he saw Clarissa in the kitchen. Her color was better and a huge smiled graced her lips as she stirred what was cooking on the stove. She seemed lost in thought and Bryce stood a moment watching her and wondering what she was thinking about. He almost felt as if he was intruding and turned to leave when Clarissa looked his way and said, "Bryce?"

"Hey, yeah, it's me. I just wanted to see how you were doing. Seems like things are going well." He nodded towards the back of the house to the boys.

Clarissa dropped the spoon and headed towards Bryce with her arms extended. She grabbed him in a hug so tight that he felt his ribs settle. "Thank you."

"You're welcome. I'm glad everything worked out okay. How's the arm?"

"Thanks to you, Tim, and Dan. I talked to Dan yesterday and he's moving to Hawaii to teach. Did you know that? The arm is fine."

"Yep, he's always wanted to live there.

Figured now was as good as a time as ever. The job made him appreciate some things. Anyway, listen I have something I wanted to do. Do you have a moment?"

"Of course."

"Okay, hang on. I'll be right back."

Clarissa went back to stirring the food until she heard footsteps behind her. When she turned around she saw Bryce and a smaller version of him standing to his left. She smiled and moved toward Bryce, "Is this...."

"Clarissa, this is my son, Glenn. Glenn, this is Mrs. Hadonfield."

"Brenner. I'm Brenner now. It's my maiden name. Hi, Glenn. I'm very pleased to meet you. I've heard a lot of wonderful things about you."

"Thank you, ma'am."

"Sean and Jeremy, can you guys come out here." Clarissa smiled at Bryce. "Please stay for dinner. I've got more than enough for all of us."

Bryce shook his head, "No we don't want to impose. I just wanted you to meet him."

"I insist Bryce Brightman. Go wash your hands, Glenn."

Ten minutes later there was a table full of men ready to dive into the meatloaf, mashed potatoes, and green beans sitting in front of them. Clarissa paused and lifted her glass, "A toast gentleman. To Bryce, thanks for helping me get my family back. To you boys, never forget that power and control can be a disease that wrenches control of your life. Be loyal, be filled with integrity, and never lose sight of who you are."

Bryce and Clarissa's eyes met as they clinked their glasses. Their boys never noticed a thing.

THE END

YOU WERE THRILLED BY THE X
YOU'RE GONNA LOVE
THE NEXT NOVEL BY LORENA BATHEY...

Coaster

The man shifted his position and set the binoculars on the ground. He opened a cooler and pulled out a beer, popped the top, and took a long drink. He smiled in anticipation. It was different than the smiles happening below him. He set the beer down next to his chair, stood, and stretched. He let out a huge yawn then sat back down to resume watching the park. Today would be spectacular. He'd spent so much time working out the details he was certain the event would go off seamlessly. He stopped and looked through the binoculars watching three teenage girls heading for the entrance to the coaster. They were followed by a family where the mother was fussing over her kids. The man moved the binoculars higher locating the track and finding the point he had marked so only he would know what was there. The track vibrated with the first riders. He was so excited he thought he might have to piss.

******

Rachel McBride pushed the sunscreen toward her daughter, Vanessa. Vanessa gave her a dirty look and pushed the sunscreen away, all while furiously texting.

"Vanessa, put this on. You don't want to burn." Rachel pushed it at her again.

"Mom, seriously? I'm not going to burn."

Her dad intervened. "Vanessa, do what your mother says. Now. And put that phone away for the day or I will take it from you for a month. Am I clear?"

Vanessa looked at her dad knowing that he was always deadly serious and losing her phone meant she wouldn't be able to talk to Josh. She closed the phone, tucked it into her pocket, and wiped the sunscreen on her legs.
Rachel mouthed, thank you to her husband.

Mitch McBride smiled at his wife. Being on vacation while visiting his in-laws was not his idea of a real escape, but at the moment it was the best he could do. He was working a deal with a huge music company to use his recording software which had allowed him to combine a vacation with business. The added bonus of doing both meant he could write the entire trip off. He could also get relief from his in-laws by saying he had 'business' when actually he just went down to the beach to chill. His in-laws were okay, but staying at their house with the kids was not the kind of relaxation he needed. He wished he could take Rachel on a cruise or go to Italy like she wanted and if he got this deal he could. For now, they were having some fun as a family. Rachel's parents immediately begged off going to the amusement park but said they would have a bar-b-que at the house later. Mitch watched his son Michael checking out the girls in line. He couldn't really fault him for it as there was a lot of skin exposed today. He glanced at a woman a few rows over with her shorts barely covering her ass and smiled. He looked, but never touched. He loved his wife. She was a beautiful woman in the way he felt a woman should be. She was curvy, smart, strong, and funny and they had been in love for over twenty years. He counted himself lucky since most of his friends had either been divorced or got caught cheating, while he still had a happy home life.

"Dad, how fast do you think that ride goes?" Michael's focus had shifted from girls to gears as he watched the coaster's angles and speed.

"Michael, put this on." Rachel handed him the sunscreen.

Michael was different than Vanessa. Instead of balking, he just did what his mother told him immediately to save an argument or being hassled. He was a smart kid and knew how to work his mom. Mitch smiled. He was proud of him even if he could be a little lazy and stubborn.

"Michael, rub it in." Rachel was almost done with sunscreen duty. She sighed and looked at the three girls standing in front of them. The girls were about eighteen, pretty, and all of them were texting while talking to each other. What was with these kids? They were constantly texting. Rachel wasn't sure that they weren't texting each other as they stood there. But she stared at their long, perfect legs feeling just the smallest twinge of regret.

Mitch put his hand on her back and leaned in to whisper in her ear.

"You're the most beautiful woman here."

Rachel smiled and kissed his cheek whispering, "I love you." He always seemed to know when she needed to hear something sweet. I guess that is what true love did for you. Immediately, she took his hand and shifted her focus back to her family.

*****

Anne Richfield looked at the map and studied the layout. Her brother was standing close and plotting what they should ride next. Christopher was tall and lanky. He was twenty but seemed a lot younger than that. Anne was the confident one who insisted that they go to the amusement park while visiting Southern California. If it was up to him they would have spent every moment driving through Beverly Hills to look at the star's homes. She had followed him through the studio tours and walked through some seedier parts of town so he could get pictures of his favorite actor's stars in the sidewalk. She was ready to laugh and scream, so here they were. Los Angeles was more Christopher's domain. But next week they would be up in San Francisco where she could wander through the streets, eat in fantastic restaurants, and check out the bohemian side of California.

"Anne, are you scared?" Christopher looked a bit nervous.

"No, are you?" Anne really didn't need to ask him but she was a bit annoyed with him. "Chris, don't be a wimp."

"I'm not. I just...I don't know..." Christopher trailed off.

"We're moving." Anne noticed a big gap and they followed behind the family in front of them.

"Can you imagine Mum and Dad on this ride?" Christopher started laughing.

The image of Diana and James Richfield on a roller coaster was completely hilarious and Anne began laughing. "That is an image."

Anne's parents were British aristocracy, at least her mother was, and being reckless was not ever part of their life. That was the reason that Chris was so uptight because their parents believed in the qualities of the elite and expected their children to do the same. Anne didn't know how to fit into the family as she longed for freedom, excitement, and the chance to experience the world.

While you would expect freedom with all the money and privilege they had, it was really more of a prison formed by rules, decency, and titles. Anne smiled as she saw the father in front of them put his hand on his wife's back and whisper in her ear. Obviously whatever he said had touched her, because her eyes were filled with gratitude and love as she leaned in and kissed him. Anne wished she'd ever seen that kind of look exchanged between her parents, or for that matter, anyone she knew. She hadn't and didn't believe she ever would. "Come on, Anne. They're moving."

*****

Roger Merit walked through the back area of the park. The corporation hid a lot of the mechanics so the park attendees wouldn't see it. There were tunnels and gates that ran through the park which made the maintenance staff almost invisible. This was carefully structured because the corporation believed that it made people nervous to see mechanics walking around the park in uniform. The perk was they also built an area for them to eat and take smoke breaks in.

Most of their work was done in the early morning hours anyway, so they didn't have a lot to do during park hours. The coasters were run by computer and were constantly monitored by staff hidden away in offices behind bathrooms or over restaurants. They needed the mechanics for the nuts and bolts, especially the older coasters that needed more maintenance. There were tough restrictions in place for the parks and the corporation had such astronomical insurance costs that attention to everything mechanical was fervent.

Roger had been an employee of the park since he was seventeen. He began working there every summer. After he got hurt playing football his scholarship went down the tubes so he just continued working at the park. He stayed until he went away to the Army. After four years he came back older, sad, and with shrapnel in his leg. He went back to the park because it seemed like a place with not much stress and the chance to work outdoors. Roger's dad had been in construction so Roger knew a lot about machines, building things, and how to handle himself around tools. That made it an easy progression to work his way to lead mechanic. He liked the job because most people were happy when they were visiting the park. He loved working on the massive machinery and the tracks the coasters ran on. The park employees that had been there a long time were like family and they looked out for each other. The corporation had restructured a few times, but usually the higher ups were the only ones that felt the change.

Roger was heading to the water ride to fix a leak that was causing water to hit the guests as they stood in line. As he maneuvered through the back walkways he thought about his morning checkout. Everything had gone smoothly and he'd spent some extra time at the highest point on their biggest coaster just enjoying the feel of the wind on his face and watching the sun rising in the sky. It was one of the perks of his job.

Walking past the new coaster he noticed the line was long. He glanced at the trio of teenage girls and was reminded of his daughter, Tori. They were giggling, texting, and so very young, he smiled in spite of himself. As he watched them, one girl jumped off the railing and headed out of the line. The two other girls yelled and the third girl with long brown hair waved. Two teenagers that were dressed alike caught his eye since that told him they must be foreign. First, because no American kids would dress alike and second, because they were incredibly pale. It was fun to watch the people, especially since they couldn't see him looking at them. Roger's radio crackled and he turned it down as he got to the water ride.

*****

The man on the hill could tell by the position of the sun and the heat that the time was nearing. Yells and screams from below were louder now as the park was near full capacity. He felt his heart beating with excitement as his plan was about to come to fruition. He took his watch out of his backpack and observed the minutes tick by. He had set the detonation for a specific time so he wouldn't have to push anything and could just absorb the joy of the spectacle below him.

He couldn't stop smiling. It had been a long haul and the planning had been not only meticulous, but really perfect. He knew that his device hadn't been found, because the ride had been running all morning. Now that it was around one o'clock he knew that people were in full ride mode and that the lines were long below him.

He stood up feeling antsy and looked at his watch to see there were only five minutes until his fulfillment came. He opened the cooler and looked at the second bottle of beer waiting. The man wasn't concerned about getting away because no one could see him this removed from the park and his camouflage clothing and accessories would keep him from view. He knew he'd have about an hour to watch the aftermath before heading to his car and back to the hotel room.

*****

Rachel and Mitch were in the first line and Vanessa and Michael first in the line next to them so they could all ride at the same time. They were watching the process before them. The ride would stop and everyone got off as the next group sat down and attached the shoulder harness to the harness between their legs. Only eight people could ride at a time, which was one of the reasons the line was so long. By the looks on the faces of people getting off, it was worth the wait.

Vanessa and Michael were teasing Rachel asking if she was going to barf. Rachel laughed knowing that she had an iron clad constitution and it was more likely that Mitch would throw up before her, but she didn't say that out loud.

To the left the brother and sister were also first in line. The boy seemed nervous as he caught Rachel's eye. She smiled at him. He nodded but quickly looked away and Rachel was pretty sure that she had embarrassed him by seeing what he was feeling. She had to admit she was a bit nervous too. She took Mitch's hand and he squeezed it. He leaned over and said, "You nervous?"

*****

Heather and Megan were next to the boy and his family. Heather was still trying to catch the boy's eye and thought he had smiled at her as they waited their turn.

Megan turned to Heather. "Lindy isn't gonna make it. They won't let her up here. She's gonna have to wait in line all over again."

Heather shrugged her shoulders, "She shouldn't have left to pee. I mean we waited a freaking hour and a half and then she leaves. Seriously? She should've gone earlier."

"I know, but now she's gonna make us stand in line again." Megan flipped her phone out. "Wait, she's texting me. She said they won't let her catch up with us so she'll be waiting at the exit. Have fun and wave to her."

*****

Lindy was pissed at herself. She had been sitting in line for so long and they had just had those frozen lemonades and she couldn't hold it any longer. She should've gone earlier, but after she got back to the line Heather and Megan were too far and the security guard grabbed her and told her she'd have to go to the end. She tried to explain her friends were up there, but he didn't care. He made her leave the line and told her to go wait at the exit for them. So now she stood here watching everyone come off the ride with huge smiles and exclamations of how cool the ride was and how scared they were. "Damn it." Lindy whispered under her breath. She texted Megan. Megan said they were getting onto the ride and they'd see her in a minute.

*****

Sitting in the ride was weird and Rachel felt like she was in a straight jacket. She was backward so she couldn't see anything. She strained her neck to see Mitch and he smiled at her. "Ready?"

Rachel tried to see the kids behind her but she couldn't so she yelled, "Hey guys, have fun. See you at the end."

"K, mom." Vanessa yelled.

Michael yelled back, "Don't yak on us."

*****

Christopher and Anne waited quietly. They felt the park worker pull on their restraints and Anne felt her heart beat quickly. She was scared. She would never tell Christopher that, but she knew it was true. Her hands were sweaty and she could feel a metallic taste in her mouth. But that didn't hide the exhilaration she felt at being scared. It was a bit intoxicating. She looked at Christopher, he simply looked panicked.

*****

The thumbs up meant the ride could move. Slowly it creeped out from the building and made its way up the hill. The full force of the sun beat down on the occupants. Sitting backwards everyone was straining their necks and a lot of silent prayers were being sent up. The creaking and clicking of the metal below the riders kept them focused, but most of them felt their mouths getting dry. As they reached the pinnacle of the climb they looked out at the park below them. They were so high up that many of them felt a horrible sinking feeling in their stomachs. With the momentary pause fear seeped in and the ride lurched and swung them back towards the ground at almost eighty miles an hour. In a chorus a scream went up.

Several of the riders began to smile while many held their face in a terrified grimace hoping that two minutes would go by fast. As they made the next turn there was a click. They all heard it, but it was lost in screams and the other mechanical sounds going on. In less than a breath there was an explosion. Instantly, it felt like someone was pouring fire on them. The heat was puzzling. Confusion was combining with pain as the car was propelled upward into the coaster's structure. Those that had figured out something was wrong were screaming, not the scared screaming of exhilaration but the desperate scream of fear. The impact was fast and when they collided with the towering metal above them the pain of being burnt was forgotten as they were crushed. Their screaming stopped.

Below the car the heat from the fire bent the metal of the tracks. The car with the people riding in it hit the metal and all forward movement stopped. The shock of metal slamming into metal caused immediate death for those where the explosion had failed.

The riders were gone and the world had changed for all those that knew them.

Coaster by Lorena Bathey
A Character Study of Grief and Loss

Coming soon
Sign up at www.LorenaBBooks
to find release date and reserve your copy.

Acknowledgements

To my family who always loves and supports me. Thank you for letting me follow my passion.

To April for reading, re-reading, and re-re-reading this book to make sure it was perfect.

To Josh for taking my ideas and making them real. You rock!

To the book bloggers and supporters of Indie Authors, thanks for taking a chance on us and sharing our work.

To Terry, thank you for making me see that being superwoman is way overrated. Thank you most for loving me.

Lorena Bathey attended St. Mary's College in Moraga graduating with a degree in English. Lorena Bathey was introduced to Marissa, Andrea, Lily, Deidre and Beatrice and her first novel, *Beatrice Munson*, came to life. After finishing the book she was inspired to write more novels and she knew that pursuing her passion was the best way to live her life.
So a writer she became.

After meeting the love of her life, they embarked on the thrilling life to follow their dreams bringing their families along for the ride.
Today Lorena has nine novels in her writing queue.

Other books by Lorena Bathey
Happy Beginnigs: How I Became My Own Fairy Godmother
Beatrice Munson
House on Plunkett Street

CPSIA information can be obtained at www.ICGtesting.com
Printed in the USA
BVOW081458060213

312492BV00001B/1/P